The Man who Lights the Stars

and other festive stories

Edited by Antonica Eikli

Ink & Locket Press

First edition

ISBN 978-1-912159-07-9

The Man who Lights the Stars

and other festive stories

M. Amelia Eikli

To Mamma and Mormor

Contents

The most expensive shoes in the world

Very few people had heard of Pietrovich. It was such a small and inconspicuous village that even if you'd passed right through it on your travels, you may not have noticed it at all. It lay deep in the forest, a few days' ride from the nearest town and a full week from the nearest city.

The villagers liked it this way. They had everything they needed, or so they felt, and thought themselves better than city folks for understanding that a little was more than enough.

The cobbler, master Nikolev, was the only man who dreamed of bigger things. He dreamed of making shoes they'd wear on the streets of St. Petersburg and Paris. He could imagine the soft leather between his fingers, and how he'd shape it into the most beautiful buttoned boots for the women and sturdy marching shoes for the men. But although he dreamed of fame, and longed to make shoes so expensive he wouldn't have wanted to wear them himself, master Nikolev stayed in Pietrovich.

He was a good man with a pure heart, and the village was full of people who needed shoes that would last. *And who else will make them shoes?* thought Nikolev. *Who else would come to the place no one remembered, only to cobble shoes for people who can't pay what they're worth?*

He was well known for his craft. His reputation declared him the best cobbler in the three districts, and he'd once had an apprentice come all the way from the city to learn from him. But when he saw master Nikolev accepting beetroots and potatoes, flower seeds and – once – half an apple for his shoes, the apprentice had been so outraged that master Nikolev asked him to leave.

"They pay what they can," he had tried to explain. "A rich merchant may pay many rubles for a pair of shoes, but the money will be a mere layer of dust on the top of his pile. He won't even notice it's gone. These people give me their food and the shirts off their backs. I'm selling the most expensive shoes in the world. They cost my customers a bit of their lives."

But despite loving his village, he loved his son more. And his son was not going to rot away out here like his father, master Nikolev thought. He taught the boy to read and write, taught him the stories and songs of the area, and when the boy knew everything his father could teach him, master Nikolev wrote to a priest in the city who agreed to take him in and send him to school.

The boy was only twelve, and although he wasn't leaving until the next morning, master Nikolev already missed him. He missed him with a pain like a toothache, somewhere deep in his heart – cycling between insistent but dull, then shooting and raw.

The priest needed the boy's help for the holy days. And since they wouldn't see each other for a long while, master

Nikolev had promised his son they would celebrate Christmas together, tonight, on the first of December. He had gotten a tree, and filled it with turtle doves, perforated hearts and angels he'd cut out of leather scraps. They had gotten 12 thin candles out of the leftover wax from the year, and tonight they would light them all, while eating the Christmas duck.

Nikolev was just about to lock the shop door and go up to begin preparing their feast, when he heard a soft knock.

"Hello?" he said through the cracks in the wood, but no one replied. *I must have imagined it*, he thought, but just as he turned the key, he heard the knock again.

"Hello?" he said again. "Who is knocking on the first night of December? We are closed. Can you come again tomorrow?" But again, he got no reply. He unlocked the door and opened it slowly, ready to slam it shut if there were robbers on the other side. Not that the door would do much good. The hinges were so worn you could break through the door by leaning on it.

"I need shoes," a voice whispered from the ground. It was a woman. Thin and pale in the freezing snow.

"Come in, child! Come in! You can't lie here like this! Let me give you a cup of tea." He helped her inside. She was barefoot, he noticed, but her feet were soft and clean, not rough and hard like someone who was used to braving the streets without shoes.

"Did someone steal your shoes, my child?" master Nikolev asked. She seemed to think about this for a long time. Nikolev found this odd – surely that was something you'd remember? Eventually, she nodded.

"Someone did steal my shoes. A long time ago. And far from here," she said. Then she cleared her throat, and her voice was large and firm when she spoke again. "Dear master cobbler, I beg you to make me a pair of good shoes.

Walking shoes. I cannot pay you right now, but I promise to come back and repay you with a great gift."

Master Nikolev smiled at her, used to people promising future gifts they couldn't offer. "Tomorrow, my dear, I will make you a pair of shoes. But tonight, will you join me and my son for a Christmas celebration? He is leaving tomorrow, and –"

"No," she said, sitting up. "It has to be tonight. I have to go. I can only stop for a very short time, or things that are whole will be broken." She looked worried. "If you cannot help me, master cobbler, I will have to leave on my bare feet, and so it will be."

Master Nikolev bit his lip. She was very young, and her skin was still blue from the cold outside. He couldn't let her leave like this, but he also didn't want to lose any time with his son on their last night together in months. He looked around his shelves and saw a pair of walking shoes that were half-finished. The order wasn't due for another week, and he'd have time to start a new pair for the baker's wife. It would be quicker to resize those for the girl than starting a whole new pair, he thought.

"All right," he sighed. "Let me see what I can do." He measured her feet and got to work. As much as he wanted to finish early, he did everything in its proper way. Every stitch lay where it was supposed to, and every fold was smoothed down thrice. The hours ticked away on the old clock behind him, and it was just past midnight when he was finally done.

"Here you go," he said, watching her try them on.

"Thank you master cobbler, these are good shoes. They will last me a long time." Master Nikolev knew this to be true, so he just smiled. "I will be back with your gift... but not too soon," she said, staring out into the air again with a curious expression, as if catching herself remembering something that hadn't yet happened. Nikolev laughed, although he was feeling quite sad.

"If you don't mind," he said, "I will go and spend the few hours I have left with my son before he leaves. I'm glad I could help you, and I wish your roads to be short and easy to tread, and your days to be long and full of happiness."

She touched his cheek lightly, and Nikolev felt his age lie thick as ice across the well in his heart.

Little Andrej had fallen asleep at the kitchen table, clutching a half-decorated gingerbread man. Nikolev rustled his hair, and tossed some slices of the Christmas goose in the frying pan, knowing the roasting would take too long. He stepped around on soft feet and lit all the candles on the Christmas tree. It shone with such warmth that it melted some of the glacier of age, even if just for the night. When he woke his son from slumber, there was a childish glow in the old man's eyes.

They ate and read the Christmas story, sang carols and played cards. Finally, they exchanged gifts, just as the first four bells of morning started ringing through the woods of Pietrovic. They were simple gifts. A pair of city shoes, a new shirt, a deck of cards and a Bible for Andrej.

"Good gifts for a city boy," Nikolev smiled.

Andrej had gotten his father a pack of fine paper and a set of pencils.

"How did you get this?" master Nikolev said, his voice shaking with pained happiness.

"Father Victor helped me. We ordered it from town! I had to help him do small tasks all year to afford it," the boy said. He was proud. Beaming. "It's so you can draw your shoes, and maybe write me some letters," he said, and they hugged for a long time.

"I will write you many letters. One every day if you wish."

"Maybe not *every* day," Andrej mumbled. "I'll need some time to play with my new friends too."

"Okay," his father smiled, rustling his hair again, "every other day, then."

When the coachman came to drive Andrej away, master Nikolev didn't cry. He just held the boy close for as long as he could, stroked his hair and said with a smile, "I am very glad and proud to be your father." Then he went back to his workshop, knowing he had done the best he could for him.

Soon, he started getting letters with stories of the big city. Andrej loved learning. He went to school, read difficult plays that Nikolev didn't understand, then went on to university to become a priest himself. Every year, he would come home on the first of December so they could celebrate Christmas together before he went back to his parish down south. Each time, Andrej would study his father's drawings of shoes, and ask him to show him parts of the trade. More than in any other place in his life, the boy's heart beat fast and strong in the workshop.

Sometimes, Andrej would send his father books or pressed flowers from his garden. Sometimes, he would give him some money, as Nikolev kept allowing the villagers to pay what they could.

"You make the best shoes in the country," Andrej complained once, studying the fine seams and beautiful patterns in a pair of lace-up boots. "You should charge more. You should come with me to the city. You'd be famous there." Master Nikolev began to explain but Andrej had heard it many times before. "I know, I know," he said. "You make the most expensive shoes in the world."

"They pay me a piece of their life," Nikolev nodded.

It was December again, and Nikolev was closing the door of his workshop. There had been a terrible snowstorm, and Andrej was delayed getting into town. Nikolev was worried, but staggered uneasily up the steep stairs and began their simple preparations. *So tired*, he thought. *I'm so very tired.*

When Andrej finally made it through the door, he found his father lying on the floor, barely breathing.

"Papa!" he said, pulling the old man up and carrying him over his shoulder to the bed. The man opened his eyes and blinked.

"Andrej?" he said. "You've come! You must be freezing, you look almost blue!"

The old man laughed. But then he thought of that December 30 years ago, when the young woman had come in and promised him a great gift for a pair of shoes. He thought of how he'd spent his evening making shoes instead of celebrating Christmas with his son, and he wished – for the first time in his life – that he had chosen differently.

What a curious thought, he smiled *to* himself. *Why drag up memories now, old man?* But then he looked up again, and saw that the girl was there – standing right next to his bed and smiling. Her cheeks were a healthy red now, and she was wearing a thick cape with a wool lining and a beautiful fur trim. But on her feet – as good as new – were the shoes he had made her that night.

"Who are you?" Andrej said, "How did you get in here?"

"It can't be!" master Nikolev said, his voice just a hoarse whisper. "It's not possible! I made those 30 years ago, they should be worn to shreds!" Then he looked at her, closer. "You... you look so young."

"For me, it has only been a day, master Nikolev," she said. Then she turned to Andrej. "Your father was kind to me once. He made me these shoes when I was lost in the snow. Now I'm here to repay him with a great gift."

She pulled something out of her sleeve. A yellow light

that hung in the air and filled the room with warmth. "Tonight was to be your last night," she said, her eyes reflecting the shimmering light.

"I know," Nikolev whispered. He had felt it in his bones.

"But I have talked to the villagers. I've gone far and wide. You've touched the lives of many, master cobbler. They told me about wonderful shoes. Working shoes that lasted six seasons and only cost a bushel of potatoes and some wax. Beautiful boots for a job interview in the city, that cost the cleaning of your workshop and a juicy pear. They told me about hours when you listened to the worries in their hearts, and days you let children play in your workshop when the mothers needed time.

"When I told them you were to die tonight, before getting a last Christmas with your son, they all begged me to give you some of their time. They asked me to thank you for the shoes. Together, they have given you one more day. A full day," she said, lifting the golden light up above Nikolev's head.

He could see it now, how several half-hours, some ten minutes stretches, two full hours and hundreds of single minutes were glowing together in there. The old man wept. His son held his hand firmly in his own.

"Thank you," Andrej whispered. The girl – or was she an old lady? A young woman? A fine lady, perhaps? He couldn't quite tell. But she smiled and let the light fall down through the old man's heart.

Master Nikolev sat up in bed. Looked around as if suddenly waking up from a dream. "Andrej?" he said, surprised. "You're here! Come on, my son, let's make Christmas."

They roasted the Christmas duck. They read the Christmas story, sang the carols and played cards. After dinner, they lit every candle on the Christmas tree and hugged each other for a very long time. Andrej had bought his father warm pyjamas and a pack of fine paper. He insisted he'd use it right now, this very night. Master Nikloev drew out some of the shoes he dreamed of, wrote Andrej a long letter and hid it in his Bible when he wasn't looking.

"I am very glad and proud to be your son," Andrej said as they hugged good night, and he stroked the old man's hair with the tenderness of the softest heart.

Master Nikolev died on the second of December, with his son singing carols by his side. The son would return to the village of Pietrovich the next year, move into his childhood house, and begin making shoes like his father had. At first, they were not very good shoes, truth be told, but Andrej had learned by watching the very best. With time, he became the new master cobbler in the village of Pietrovich.

As he closed the workshop every first of December, he whispered, "Merry Christmas, papa," into the night. The stars twinkled back in reply.

How puppy Number Six found his name

The puppy's name was Number Six, as he was the sixth to come out and no one was waiting for him.

"There's another, coming," the human said, "a little runt. Probably won't make it." So they didn't name him, and the lack of name stuck. The human had tried to get rid of him – put an ad in the paper and offered him for free. But it was right before Christmas, and all the children wanted puppies with wagging tails and silky ears. The adults, on the other hand, wanted puppies who'd grow big enough to come jogging and hiking, which they'd all start doing in the new year, *for sure.*

Number Six had only a stub for a tail. It would wag, of course, but it affected his hind legs – one shorter than the other – and pushed him into a rotating shuffle of excitement. He would run and play with the rest of them – the best of them – but his limp and stump made him an ill fit for the huge silk bows and gleaming children's eyes that

Christmas demanded. These concepts are far too human for a dog to understand, but still, he knew the truth of it in his little puppy heart.

It was a surprise for him then, when the human picked him up by the skin of his neck, placed him in a bag in the car, and drove him off into the world.

I get a home! the puppy thought. *A family with a cuddly lap, and a real name, too!* But what he got was a hard tumble to the side of the road, where the swish of the cars and the cold from the ground made him cower and whimper until the very next dawn.

I can't stay here, the little pup thought. *My family's out there, and they'll get worried if I don't show up soon.* A clever pup, he stayed away from the road and headed in through the trees instead. They were awfully tall, he thought, and getting taller, so he steered this way and that, walked in every direction and sometimes in none. Until suddenly, there it was! Exactly as he imagined, a back lawn stretched out in front of him, all grey and brown from frost and mud, but a lawn it was nonetheless.

"Bark!" he said, spinning in circles as his stump propelled him across the grass, "I'm home!"

An old lady sat on her garden bench, enjoying the few rays of sunshine the winter sky allowed her.

"Oh, great," she sighed, seeing the circling puppy on her lawn. "Another dog in my garden. Just what I wanted."

This is just what I wanted too! thought Number Six, and when he'd finally made it all the way over to her, he sat on his bum and looked at her with all of his heart.

"So you're the one who comes to visit, what?" she said. "My own children can't find the time to visit, but you visit just by accident, what?"

"Bark!" the puppy said, and tilted his head. "This is no accident. I came looking for you!"

"What do you want, pup?" she said, stomping her cane on the ground a few times.

"Bark!" he said. "I want to be yours!"

"Is that so?" the lady said, then closed her eyes and turned back to the sun. The puppy jumped across her foot and landed on it, sprawled across with his feet on either side.

"Bark!" he said. "Look how well I fit on your foot!"

"You still here?" she said after a while.

"Bark!" said the eager puppy. "I'll always be here!"

"Is that so?" said the woman again. "Bark bark to you, too." The puppy's heart swelled. *What a lovely thing to say*, he thought. As the old lady stood up to go inside, she stomped her cane again.

"Shoo!" she said. "Shoo! Shoo!" And the puppy danced around her legs, as he thought it was a most beautiful name.

The gap in the door was a bit too narrow, but he managed to squeeze in behind her, even so.

"Bark!" he said. "This is a great home! Oh, and look, this can be my spot!" He rolled around on a rug by the TV, and the old lady nodded to herself.

"Come here," she said, "let me have a look at you. Can barely walk. What happened to your tail, pup? Tsk. Whatever sort of use do I have for a broken dog?" She picked him up and placed him in her lap, her fingers absentmindedly scratching him behind his wonky ear.

"Bark!" he said, and licked her hand.

"I see," she said and closed her eyes, feeling the puppy's soft fur beneath her fingers. "I guess that's the wrong sort of question altogether."

By Christmas Eve, when the tree was lit and the house smelled faintly of gingerbread and anticipation, her children came to visit.

"Sorry we haven't been here for a while," they said. "We've been so busy. But we're here now, all of us, together. Isn't it nice to be a family?" And their mother nodded and smiled, and said that yes, it is nice to be a family indeed. And when the kids left the next morning, with places to be and things to do, they said to each other that it was good for their mother, that she now was a one out of two.

They waved goodbye to the pair on the porch. Their grumpy old mother and a puppy named Shoo.

The song I used to be

"What's her name, again?" said James, quickly skimming through the papers in the folder he'd been handed.

"Delores Bellingham," said the matron. "She's got no family to speak of. There's a second cousin who showed up here once, mostly to find out if there was an inheritance to be gained. Other than that, she's on her own. We don't know much about her, to tell you the truth, and she doesn't really respond much. Hardly a reaction to get, whatever we do."

"I'll see what I can find out," said James, and the matron shrugged. She knew the drill; this happened every year. A bunch of fresh holiday temps – nursing students, for the most part – would come in for the holidays, wanting to make a difference. They'd coo and coddle the old biddies for a few days, until the reality of poo and drool had time to sink in through their shirts properly.

It's probably a good thing, though, she thought. *It*

gives the old bats some extra attention for a few days, and heaven knows they don't get enough of that. She walked the young nurse to the door, gave him his final instructions and scuttled back to her desk. Two minutes later, he was out of her mind.

"Good morning, Delores," James called as he entered the dark room. The old lady moved her head towards him, slowly, her eyes not quite following suit.

Delores. The name felt familiar. It stirred in her like a stone in water, but soon, it was forgotten. What was she doing? She turned her head back to the window, let her eyes run to nothing at all and linger among the trees across the street.

"How are you today?" someone said. She turned her head towards the sound. A question. How was she today? Her skin itched. There was a dull pain somewhere in her back. And... there had been a word. Something stirring like a stone in water. She couldn't quite put her finger on it. The lake was still now.

The window. She liked the window. She'd been looking for her neighbour's house. It had been there all her life, right outside the kitchen window. They had changed it, though, and she didn't know when. It used to be a small yellow house in the middle of a field. Now it was a huge grey office block in the middle of a city. But there were some trees there, to the side. Perhaps her neighbour's house was behind that.

What had his name been? Johnny? He was four years old, she thought, so she must be six. She hadn't been there to play for days. Maybe she could ask to go play with him now.

Ah, but he was here, already. Right here in her room. Older than she remembered, but perhaps she'd just forgotten. Her hands looked older, too. *Oh yes*, she thought, *I'm old now.*

"Let's get you dressed," he said, and she smiled a little. She was a bit cold, and she seemed to still be in bed. It must be midday, at least, as brightly as the sun shone on the crisp, white snow. Snow. Snow that was cold and hard. Snow that crunched under her bare feet when she ran across the yard when dad came home. When was this? Home from the war? Where was the yard?

"What a lovely dress," said a man in her room. He held out a brown thing from a cupboard. Was it hers? She thought not. She couldn't remember ever having owned anything brown. Oh, but she did have dark red dress, somewhere. Soft velvet with a big white collar in the finest lace. Her mum had sewn it, with money from the store. Was her mum at the store? She looked around. She couldn't quite remember why she hadn't bought anything. The man in her room smiled. She smiled back. He was handsome. Reminded her a bit of George. That's right. She had married George. They didn't have any children. She had wanted children.

"Where is George?" she said. The voice that came out was soft and shaky. *I don't speak much*, she thought. She felt her throat all dry and sore, torn up by a single question.

"Who's George, Delores?" said the man in her room. He was sweet. Smiled to her. He had white scrubs on. A doctor, perhaps.

"Delores," she nodded. "I'm Delores." A picture album was in her lap. He had put it there, she thought. Was it his album? But she recognised these people. Her mother, her father, the boy next door. What was his name? Johnny?

"Who's George?" Johnny said, standing right next to

her now, all grown up. He flipped pages in her album and she saw so many faces. They were important – she felt that was true – some of them… they stirred something in her. Stones in water, making ripples across. But soon, the lake fell silent and the water still. There were trees outside the window. She liked trees. One of them had lights, under the snow. Glowing.

"Christmas," she whispered.

"Yes," said the man in her room. "It's almost Christmas! Do you like Christmas?" She nodded slowly. The word itself made her smile. Christmas. It meant something deep and definite inside her. It meant something happy. A tree with lights outside her window.

"Do you take milk in your tea, Delores?" Milk from a glass bottle on the porch, every morning. It was her job to get it in. She'd forgotten today. She should do it soon. Tea with milk before school. But maybe there would be no school as there was so much snow outside her window. Too far to walk when there was this much snow.

Her brown dress had crumbs on it. She brushed them off with an ancient hand, the movement not as precise as she expected it to be. Brown fabric with white flowers. *This used to be my favourite*, she thought. Now, there were crumbs. Ah, but no wonder. There were biscuits on a plate on the table, and tea in her mug. Good tea, too!

"Good tea," she said.

"That's good!" said the man in her room.

Tea with milk and biscuits on a plate. Just the way she liked it. An afternoon treat when George came home from work. He would sip his tea, put her feet in his lap and knead them while she read him the paper. He should be coming home from work soon. She wriggled her toes expectantly. It was getting dark. There was a tree full of light, glowing out there. Had she watered the Christmas tree? She heard a crackling.

A man stood there in the room, fiddling with a radio. She was sure she didn't know him. What was he doing here?

"Radio," she croaked, surprised by the rawness of her own voice. It must have been some time since she spoke last.

"Yes," said the man, smiling at her. He was handsome. Reminded her a bit of George. Her husband. She missed him dearly. He had died, George. When they were still so young.

"I thought you'd like some music," he said. George, her George, standing there in white scrubs. The doctors must have lent them to him after the accident. And now he was here! She smiled. The song. It was the song.

'Have yourself a merry little Christmas', oh yes! She knew this song. She loved Judy Garland. *Meet Me in St. Lewis*, wasn't that the film? It was so long ago. The melody stirred the waters. Her parents used to ask her to sing to them. She had played the piano. Oh, how she longed to play the piano. Her fingers sought the air and caressed the imagined keys. She'd played for George in the evenings. And oh, she had loved the way he looked at her then. His gentle eyes across his spectacles, admiring her on the piano. This song… they had called it the Christmas song. The. The most important one.

"You play the piano?" said a young nurse in her room. She smiled.

"I used to play the piano," she said, nodding. "I used to play the piano for my husband. George." The song was a boat on the water, carrying her across the memories on the bottom, allowing her to see them clearly. At least the ones closest to the boat. At least the ones that were here, right now.

"You look a bit like him, you know," she laughed, "he had that impish smile, just like you." She laughed again. Clucking. The sound of pebbles hitting water. She stood up with only the slightest wobble. She'd always been strong, Delores. She'd always loved to run and climb. Her body was weak now. *I sit too much*, she thought.

"Won't you dance with me?" she said. Then she cleared her voice and sang.

The matron sighed when Agatha came to get her.

"It's Mrs. Bellingham, ma'am," the young nurse said.

"What about her, is she ill?"

"No, she's... she's dancing, ma'am."

And this is what the matron saw: the old biddy, Mrs. Bellingham, swaying across the floor with the student nurse's hands around her waist. She was singing, too. A voice as brittle and thine as spun sugar, but singing she was, even so.

"Christmas music," the boy said. "She likes Christmas music. And playing the piano." The matron nodded and made a note in her journal.

"Christmas songs are often a powerful key," she nodded brusquely. She wasn't too surprised the old lady reacted to Christmas music. It happened to one or two of them every year.

"I used to sing them for my husband, George," Delores said, smiling. Her face was a new face. One the matron had never met. "He died in an accident, my George. He was so young. But he used to love my singing." The old lady beamed.

"Thank you," she said, winking at the young student and giving him a hug bordering on the inappropriate. "I think you gave me this song. Didn't you?" The song was ending, and the old lady sat down in her chair. Her face still beamed, but her eyes slowly dragged out through the window and across the car park to the other side of the road. The next song was Jingle Bell Rock, but Dolores didn't seem to notice it at all. The others looked at each other, exchanged insecure smiles.

"Make sure you dress that wound on her hand," the matron said to the student nurse. She swallowed. "She's prone to infection." She swallowed again.

"Merry Christmas, Mrs. Bellingham," she said, backing out of the door without waiting for a reply. It wouldn't come, she knew.

The matron went into her office and closed her door behind her. *Take a few deep breaths*, she thought, and promptly listened to her own advice. She sat down heavily in her chair, and began to call around for a piano.

The man who lights the stars

The sky is a ceiling; each star a lantern. All the glass is ancient, hand-rolled or thinly blown. It buckles like waves in the cast iron frames, a slight green tint where the glass is thicker, a hint of yellow at its thinnest points. Many of the panes are cracked, but none are broken. These lanterns are well cared for, their hinges regularly oiled and the glass carefully polished. The light up there is amazing. It's amazing down here, too. You see them as hundreds and thousands of stars, and you are lucky, truth be told, to be able to see them at all. But the luckiest ones, and there are very few, get to see them for what they really are: hundreds and thousands of slow-burning candles, shining just strongly enough to reflect off the sea.

Every night, a man lights the stars. He walks with a limp. He's old and grey, and he climbs his endless ladder with unsteady, wobbly steps. Every night, he strikes the flint and steel from his tinderbox until the waxed wick of his lighting pole burns. He climbs, and hopes – against all reason – that the flame won't blow out as he climbs to the sky.

He wears a coat of wonders. The pockets are full, so heavy they make him hunch over a little, and are filled with hundreds of candles, candle stubs, balls of wick and wax, a tinderbox in silver, and another one of tin. He doesn't love the coat for the pockets, however. He loves the way it keeps him warm, wraps around him even when the wind makes the heavy lanterns sway on their hooks. And he loves the two extra buttons his wife has sewn on its collar. Now, he can button it all the way up. It really helps, on the chilliest nights.

"Excuse me?" says the girl. Her voice rolls against the firmament and echoes slightly against the crystal floor. She gets no response.

"Hello?" she calls, looking up the shaking ladder. She hears something. A squeak of some sort. Perhaps she should start climbing and see if she can find him up there, but she doesn't know if this ladder will take them both, and doesn't want to do something stupid. Not on her first day.

I'd better just wait, she thinks. And so she waits. Her coat has only two pockets. One for each hand, and space for half a sandwich – and an apple, at a stretch. A star lights up above her head. *So there he is*, she thinks, her stomach aflutter.

"There we go, that's right, slowly now, one step at a time," she hears from somewhere in the air above her. The man who lights the stars is here. "A visitor? No, no, can't be, can't be a visitor. Hello?" he says as she sees her. His thick spectacles have fogged up from the climb, and his large, grimy handkerchief does nothing but spread the mist more evenly across the glasses. She hands him a yellow paper slip and tries to smile endearingly.

"Are you Mr. Luc?" she says, holding out her hand to shake his.

"Apprentice? They've sent me an apprentice? Never had an apprentice before. So young as well; can she even climb, I wonder?" Mr. Luc doesn't take her hand. He doesn't respond, either. He just mutters along as he reads the note over and over and over again.

"Mr. Luc, my name is Aurelia, and I've been sent here to learn how to light the stars before you... so you won't be the only one who knows how," she says. "...If something happens to you, or something," she continues, as he still doesn't reply. Smiling kindly, she forces her hand into his. "Lovely to meet you."

"Ah, yes, Mr. Luc's an old man, now, best be careful with ladders and flames," the old man says, studying her small hand against his, "but can she climb? Mr. Luc sure can't, no, not any longer. Here!" he says, thrusting the lighting pole into her hands.

"This is the lighting pole. It holds the fire, your tinderbox creates the flame. You *do* have a tinderbox?" he says, looking at her closely. "No tinderbox, no candles, no? Not much of a candle lighter then, I see, but she can learn, oh yes, she can learn if she can climb."

Aurelia clears her throat. "Mr. Luc, I have a tinderbox." It's the size of an apple, fits right in her pocket. It's beautifully carved in rosewood, and smells faintly of campfires everywhere. It's too big for an experienced man like Mr. Luc, but good for those who are clipping sparks for the first time.

"Oh yes, a tinderbox she has indeed, and if she can climb, she can light the stars." He grins at her.

"This is how you move the ladder," he says, and shows her the hook holding it to the floor. It's so small and laughably weak, she can't believe he trusts it to keep the ladder in place.

"Is that it?" she says as he slides the ladder over to the next hook and fastens it.

"It's enough," he says. "There you go, now, climb up and light the star."

"How?" she says.

"You'll see when you get there, it's not that hard."

She climbs slowly at first, then faster when she sees that the ladder will hold. It's cold up here, and grows colder and colder. But then she arrives among the hundreds of lanterns he's already lit. They warm the air with soft heat and the glow of a gentle Christmas fire. She unfastens the hatch at the lantern door with the hook at the end of the pole. More than half the candle remains, so she stretches until the flame touches the wick, closes the door and returns to the ground.

"What if the candle is low?" she says.

"You change it," he says, giving her a handful of candles.

"What if my light pole blows out?" she says.

"You relight it," he says, pointing to her tinderbox.

"What if the hinges groan or the glass is blackened?"

"You oil them or polish them," he says.

"What if a lantern breaks?"

"You drop it through the floor. They like a falling star every now and then."

"What if I can't light all the stars before the night is over?" she says.

"Then you try again tomorrow," he says. Then he laughs. "The largest one, the one in the middle, you only light that on Christmas Eve. Other than that, there is nothing to it. Just climb and light and climb again." She looks around. Takes in the thousands of little hooks on the floor, the criss-crossing paths from the ladder's track. She nods. It's not that hard, she realises. Not that much to learn. Endlessly repetitive. Endlessly dull. And still, she finds herself wanting to go back up. She wants to be there, in the warm yellow glow, and she wants to be there right now. She longs to be among the stars, and perhaps she always did.

She moves the ladder and climbs. When she gets to the top, she takes a breath. She's surrounded by lanterns. The lit and the dark, the cracked and the whole.

"It's beautiful!" she calls down the ladder. "It's really, really beautiful."

"I love the large lanterns with the yellow glass," she says. "And the smaller ones with just a few windows. The blue ones are nice! And this one has so many spikes... oh, I love what it does to the light!" She can reach a couple of lanterns from where she stands, and she lights them all and smiles.

The old man is gone. She knew he would be. But he's left her his coat of wonders. It fits her perfectly, although she couldn't tell you how. It's heavy, makes her slouch a little bit, and she can feel the strain on her knee as she buttons the coat all the way up, moves the ladder, and climbs.

The angel who crashed in the garden

"I'm so *bored*," Anna said, knocking her head gently against the birch in the garden. "How much longer?"

Her brother sighed and checked his watch, carefully counting the minutes left until it would be six o'clock. "Twenty-four minutes," he said.

"That's more than an *hour*," Anna said, horrified.

"No," Adam said, patiently, "it's only half as much. But it's still a very long time."

Their mum had insisted they got some air and told them to play in the garden for a while. The first stretch of time had been fine, as Adam had managed to bring his Nintendo outside, hidden under his jacket. They'd taken turns playing until the battery gave into the cold, and now, there was nothing to do.

"It's not fair," Adam mumbled. "I was out all day yesterday with class! I don't see why *I* have to be outside just because *you* need your head airing out."

"Mum said not to argue," Anna said, seeing her brother's attempt at riling her up for what it was. "Besides," she continued, as soon as she felt the moral victory was secured, "*you're* the one who wouldn't stop playing on the Xbox. It's your fault she got mad in the first place."

"It's not!" Adam said, although he knew this perfectly well to be true.

"Can we play something?" Anna said as another excruciatingly long minute passed in silence.

"Like what?"

"*I* don't know," Anna said, putting into her voice a clear suggestion that *she* was not the elder brother with all the good ideas. "Like hide and seek or something?"

Her brother scoffed. "Where would we even hide, though? You can see the whole garden from here."

"We could make up a game?" Anna suggested.

"No we couldn't, because it's too cold to think," said Adam, picking strips of bark of the tree.

"Joy to the world!" Anna began singing. It was the day before Christmas after all, and a little music was never wrong, in her opinion. Adam seemed to feel differently about it and had placed his glove-clad hand across her mouth within a second. "Oww!! Uww Huwwtng Mww!"

"Shh," he said, "I heard something."

"No you didn't," Anna spat, having bitten herself free from her brother's grip, "you just don't like it when I sing."

"No, shh, shut up," he said, waving his hand in her direction. "There it is again! Do you hear it?"

Anna scrunched up her face in a serious listening expression and tilted her head slightly. And yes, there was something there. A thin whistling sound that seemed to be growing stronger and stronger.

"It's like something's falling," she whispered.

"No, stupid. Things only make that sound when they

fall in cartoons."

Anna shrugged, about to retort when something crashed down through the roof of the Wendy house with a smashing, splintering thump.

"Guess we're in a cartoon, then," she said, looking at her broken play house, horrified at the devastation. Adam looked up. He had read about planes dropping people, luggage and toilet ice everywhere, but there wasn't a single airplane to be seen.

"We should get mum," Anna said, already heading towards the house.

"No, wait," Adam said, holding her back. "Let's check what it was first. If it's a dead person, she won't let us look at it unless we see it now."

Anna shuddered. "I don't want to see a dead person... *Adam*," she whined as her brother walked slowly towards the Wendy house "Adam, let's just get mum."

"Hnghh..." they heard from the Wendy house. "Hello?"

"Adam!" Anna whispered, "Adam! Please! Let's get mum!"

Before Adam could reply, a pale face appeared in the glass of the door. It looked confused, but not especially hurt or scary.

"Hello?" the face said. "Could you let me in please?" The siblings looked at each other.

"Eh... you're the one who's... in..." Adam said, his forehead wrinkling with semantic acrobatics. "We're outside..."

The face grinned at them. "Oh, I'm sorry," it said. "Would you let me out then, please?"

"I don't know if we should," Anna hissed. "What if it's a cat burglar?"

Adam rolled his eyes. "What is it with you and cat burglars? It's not a cat burglar, okay?"

"You don't know!" Anna protested. "He... she landed on her feet and isn't hurt! Sounds like a cat to me..."

"Are you a cat burglar?" Adam asked the face in the door.

"No?" the face replied, and Adam pointed at it while looking at his sister.

"See?" He opened the door and stepped back quickly, as if worried the person in there would rush at him. The door slid open slowly, but the person seemed to make no move to step out.

"Eh... it's open," Adam said.

"Oh! I see! It's like a ground opening?" the person said, stepping through with unsure steps.

"Excuse me," Anna said, "are you... are those... did you fly here?" she said, then gathered some courage. "Actually, excuse me, but like, are you an angel?" she said.

The person in front of them – a young boy or girl – was wearing a white robe and had a pair of what could only be described as wings poking out into the air. Soft, long feathers rustled gently in the wind, and although there was a definite disheveled air from the fall, the person still looked strangely pure and beautiful.

"Don't be stupid," Adam scolded his sister. "Of course it's not an angel."

"Yes!" the angel said. "Of course I am! I'm Mazraphael, angel of the Lord, bringer of good news and tidings from God!"

They looked at each other. Adam swallowed, unsure what to say.

"Happy to meet you," Anna said eventually, then curtsied, just to be safe. She had never met an angel before.

"Eh..." Adam said, chewing his lip. "Are you a boy or a girl?"

"I think so," the angel nodded, "but I'm not sure I fully

understand the difference."

Adam and Anna exchanged glances. "It doesn't matter," Adam said. "Nice to meet you."

"Nice to meet you too," the angel said enthusiastically, stretching its huge wings out into the air. "Ow!" it howled. "That really hurt!" Mazraphael huddled together as if struck, and one wing seemed to bend at an unfortunate angle.

"Might be broken," Adam said, nodding seriously. "Looks like that pigeon we found, remember?"

Anna paled. "Do you think Dad will break its neck?" she whispered.

The angel shot up. "Oh, please no!"

"No, no, no, of course not. Don't listen to her," Adam said reassuringly. "You can't wring the necks of people unless you're in the army, and dad's not in the army. He's an accountant." The angel seemed to relax at this news, as the lack of physical intimidation from accountants is a universal truth.

"Can you point me to the fields, please? I'll be late soon," the angel said.

"There's a field right there," Adam said, pointing over the fence to the Henderson's pasture.

"Don't *think* that's it," the angel said, pondering the view. "Are there any shepherds there?"

Anna shook her head. "Shepherds look after sheep," she said.

"And those are...?" the angel said, smiling apologetically.

"Cows," Anna said, "cattle."

"Cowscattle," the angel said. "Of course, I see it now." The siblings looked at each other again.

"You're not from England, are you?" Adam said, well versed in the strange ways of foreigners.

The angel laughed, a sound like trumpets and chimes in

the air. "Of course not!" it said, "I'm from heaven."

"Right," Adam said, nodding. Then, having learned quite a bit about small talk from his father, he said, "How has your country reacted to Brexit?"

The angel smiled. "It's kept us busy, all the prayers, but we think our side will get the advantage back any day now." Then it seemed to blush. There was an air of PR about its words that went right above Anna's head, but Adam had just been allowed to start watching the news and recognised a politician when he saw one.

"Right," he said shortly.

"I really need to get going," the angel said, scratching its forehead. "Is there a field with shepherds around? It should be right outside Bethlehem," it said.

"Bethlehem the school? There are no fields around there."

"Not a school... it's a town," the angel said.

"No... it's a school," Adam said. "We both go there."

The angel snapped its fingers and a scroll of paper appeared in its hand.

"No, see here," Mazraphael said, "'In the little town of Bethlehem, head out to the large fields. Shepherds will be living there, keeping an eye on their flocks. An angel of the Lord –', that's me," Mazraphael said, smiling humbly, "'– will appear before them and say...'"

"Oh..." Adam said, "you've got the wrong Bethlehem... and I'm... I think you're a bit late." He looked to Anna, who nodded gravely.

"Oh no!" said the angel. "Has it already happened? Who did they send instead? I bet it was Zukhanael, wasn't it? They've been trying to steal my role for centuries now..." The angel sat down in the air as if onto a chair and hovered there, without the slightest concern for the insubstantial support.

"I've practiced so much!" the angel said. "Do you want to see?"

"Eh... sure," Anna said, patting Mazraphael's hand, "you show us, I'm sure you're *really* good."

"FEAR NOT!" the angel shouted, stretching its arms out into the air. The kids startled.

"That's a bit much," Adam said. "It's a bit scary... you know... if you don't expect it."

The angel's face fell. "It is? How about this? Fear NOT!" it said, with a slightly different intonation. Louder, but less abrupt.

"Eh, yes, that's better," Adam said.

"I've come to bring you WONDERFUL news!" the angel beamed. "You're gonna be so EXCITED! Like... it's the BEST THING that has ever happened on this little planet, and you should just – GAAH!! I can't even – that's how... you know, it's just SO COOL!" Anna and her brother gaped. This was not what they remembered.

"That's strange," the angel said, slightly puzzled, "I've never said things like that before. Normally, it's just, 'Hail thee, shepherds of Bethlehem, I come bearing great tidings of joy and peace for the world!'" The kids giggled at the angel's contorted voice.

"Maybe it's 'cause you're here," Adam reasoned. "It's like... it's the way you'd sound if you were going to speak to people today."

"What do you mean?" the angel said.

"Well... Jesus was born 2,000 years ago, right? So..." Adam said.

"What?!" the angel said, suddenly standing ten inches above the ground. "I'm *2,000 years* late?"

"Well... Duhh," Anna said, rolling her eyes. "*Everyone* knows that."

"I missed it," the angel said, sinking even further down

into its invisible chair. "I missed the choir... I missed the message... I missed the big day completely!"

The angel sobbed. Big tears fell and exploded into showers of glitter on the ground.

"Oh, don't cry," Anna said, patting the angel's hand again. "I'm sorry." The angel sniffed.

"Hey," Adam said, scratching his head. "How long did it take you to get here?" he said. "Like... can't you just go back to the right time, like you were supposed to?"

The angel shook its head. "No, because I can only be one place at any one time. This is Christmas Eve, and obviously, I can't be both here on Christmas Eve and in Bethlehem on Christmas Eve 2,000 years ago."

"Well *obviously* not," Adam said, a tad testily. "But Jesus wasn't really born on Christmas Eve, was he?" he said.

"What?" said the angel.

"What?" said Anna.

"No, really. I read about it one of dad's journals," Adam pushed on. "It said that if Jesus was real –"

"Of course he's real!" the angel said, horrified.

"Of course he is," Anna said, patting its hand and sending her brother a strict look.

"– then his real birthday was more likely in March or April," Adam continued, unperturbed. "So if you can get back to the right time, then you can still make the actual day."

"Oh! Great!" the angel said, starting to fly off, then collapsing as its wing gave in. "Ohnfh..."

"Yes... your wing looks a bit... broken," Adam said. "Our mum is a nurse..." He bit his lip again while thinking. "But I'm not sure she knows how to treat angels. Maybe a veterinarian would be better? Like... since you've got wings like a bird, I mean," he said apologetically.

"Maybe we should ask mum first," Anna said, worried that their mum wouldn't get to see the angel in their garden.

Adam shrugged. "Worth a try," he said, pointing the angel in the direction of the door then stopping to check the time. "Actually, we should wait another... four minutes before we go in. We're grounded," he added, as the angel seemed confused.

"What?" the angel said, its question just a thin gust of breath. "Is that why you don't have any wings? You have to stay on the ground?"

Adam laughed. "No, we just broke her exercise bike when we were playing fort the other day, so we have to play outside every day and not play Xbox all the time."

"Unfair, really," Anna added. "She never used that bike anyway."

The minutes passed as Adam tried to explain to Mazraphael the concepts of both an Xbox and an exercise bike, but at two seconds past six, they stepped inside.

"Mu-u-um?" Anna called. "An angel crashed in the garden!"

"That's great, hon. Dinner will be ready in five!" their mum called from the kitchen.

"No, it's really hurt!" Anna called, "It needs help!"

"I swear, if you've brought another pigeon insi..." their mum said, wiping her hands as she stepped into the hall, then stopped dead at the sight of the angel.

"FEAR NOT!" Mazraphael said, "I've come to deliver just the BEST NEWS, like I can't even –"

"Eh, maybe not right now," Adam said, seeing his mum's face drain of blood. "Mum, just chill, okay? It's okay. It's just lost. But it's wing is –"

"I'm going to call the police!" their mum said, holding her small kitchen knife out in the air in front of her and waving at the kids to get behind her.

"Oh, good!" the angel said, smiling. "They're like official helpers, aren't they?"

"Mum," Adam sighed, "it's a real angel. I checked. Mazraphael, show her your back," he said.

The angel obediently turned around, the torn robe revealing the place where wings sprouted from its shoulder bones.

"Oh... Oh my..." their mum whispered.

"And one of them's broken, or something," Anna said, pointing to the place where the wing shot to the side.

"I'm not sure..." their mum said, then shook her head a little. "Okay. Sit down, Mr. Angel, and let me take a look."

Mazraphael sat down in the air again, hovering just slightly lower than where a normal chair would be.

"Okay," their mum said again, approaching the angel slowly. She touched its wings with careful fingers, identifying where the feathers became skin, and the underlying bone structure.

"I'm not sure it's broken, Mr. Angel," she said. "It feels like the bone here has come out of its socket... We could probably take you to the hospital to make sure... but I'm not certain it would be a good idea. How... how easily do you heal? Don't you have any magic or anything like that?" She blushed at her own question.

"I don't know," the angel said. "Don't think any of us has broken one of our wings before."

"Right..." she said. "Okay, well... If you're happy to try, I'll attempt to set it for you. This is going to hurt. Are you ready?"

"I'm ready," the angel said, clutching the invisible seat it was sitting on for support. There was a loud snap and a groan from the angel.

"How does that feel?" their mother said nervously.

"Better!" the angel said, stretching its wings out

completely. "Oh, that's great! Thank you!"

"You... you're welcome."

"Okay," Adam said, "I think the journal is still in dad's study, I'll go find it. Mum, can Mazraphael stay for dinner?"

"Uhm, sure... Do you eat pork?" their mother asked, then brought the angel into the kitchen while trying to explain why they would eat animals when they could choose not to. When Adam came to join them, the angel was chewing happily on a pork chop with cheese and apple sauce.

"I get it now," it said, pointing at its food with a half-bent fork. "It's delicious!"

Adam read the article to them as they ate, and they all agreed there was a very good chance the angel would still make the real Christmas Eve.

"Just remember to be a bit less frightening," Anna said. "I got really scared when you shouted in my face like that. Maybe try to say, like, 'Don't be scared!' instead. It's easier to understand."

"Thank you, I will try," Mazraphael said, giving her the awkward hug of someone who's never tried hugging before.

"Good luck," Adam said, holding out his hand to shake the angel's.

"Thank you," it said, holding its hand out in the air in the same way. They all smiled, but no one corrected the handshake. It looked right enough for the situation.

"Be careful with that wing," their mother said sternly. "It seems fine now, but be careful."

"I will," the angel said, smiling. "Thank you very much for helping me."

"Give Baby Jesus a kiss from me," she said, laughing at the very thought.

"I will!" the angel said. "All right... I guess I'm off!" it said, and that was it. Suddenly, the angel just wasn't there.

When their dad came home, they were all a bit fuzzy on the details. They felt something important had happened, but couldn't quite remember what. Their mother said Anna and Adam had been playing in the garden, pretending to be the angels that had come to bring tidings to the shepherds on the fields of Bethlehem.

"And somehow, they fell through the roof of the Wendy house," she said, wrinkling her forehead as she couldn't quite understand how they got up there in the first place. "Luckily, they're both unhurt," she said, although she felt she could remember the cracking of bone.

The next morning, their eyes still groggy with sleep and alight with the joy of new clothes and toys, the kids sat down around the breakfast table, ready for their father to read the Christmas story, like he always did.

"And there were shepherds living in the fields nearby," he read, and the children winked at each other across the table. "But the angel said to them, 'Do not be afraid!'" he continued, and Anna, Adam and their mum began to laugh.

"What's so funny?" he said, a bit annoyed to be interrupted in this way.

"I don't know," their mum said, laughing again. "It's just such a good line. Subtle."

"I like it," Anna said.

"Me too," Adam said. And then they listened as their father finished reading, filled with Christmas cheer and joy. Soon, grandma and grandpa would come over. Soon, they would sing carols and eat Christmas pudding. Today would be a great day.

No one watched as, outside the window, soft flakes of snow began to cover up specks of glitter on the lawn.

Christmas in the city

Christmas in the city means people, people, people. And I miss you more in this crowd than I do between all the tourists of summer. Perhaps it's the way everyone is wrapped up in coats and scarves, hats and mittens. The layers of clothing that pad them out and turn them into strangers that could be you. The fact that you *could* be here makes me forget that I'm glad you aren't, and it feels just like missing you, although I know it isn't. Or perhaps it's the way they're all rushing around to find presents for loved ones, and how the lights from the Christmas decorations reflect off their eyes like glitter. It reminds me of the way you used to smile when I laughed, and of how I became glitter in your eyes. It makes me think of how we always gave people the best presents. Even when we couldn't afford to. It makes me think of you, that's all.

So I miss you, in the city, when it's Christmas and too many people. But for the most part – the rest of the year

– I'm so relieved to be here alone. Sometimes, I go into bars and chat to strange people about personal things. We're a throng now, around Christmas, we who want to find someone we can 'may I just tell you something?' and 'another thing I've never told anyone before...' our hearts out to. We recognise each other by our tear-streaked city faces. Like we're covered in warpaint of salt and dust, preparing for a battle against ourselves and the season.

Heartache in the city means lonely, lonely, lonely. But the city itself wraps around me and tells me it has something up its sleeve. The Christmas lights lead me around another corner, where a hundred thousand strangers – all in coats, scarves, mittens – could be another you, only better. I buy myself hot chocolate and play 'one-two-three to marry', listen to 'Rockin' Around the Christmas Tree' for the nineteenth time today on the shopping centre stereo. I watch people ice skate in the city square and drop a few pounds in the Salvation Army's collection bucket, although I know there are plenty of reasons not to. I find myself in The Works, buying a huge stack of Christmas cards, and I write one to everyone whose address I know – including the prime minister – but not to you. I send them with wishes for a happy holiday season and a sensible new year.

December in the city means music, music, music. Everywhere plays 'All I Want for Christmas is You' and 'Jingle Bell Rock', but I drown it all out with 'Have Yourself a Merry Little Christmas' and 'O Holy Night'. Nat King Cole, Frank Sinatra, Judy Garland and Sarah McLachlan walk with me, keep me company through the crowded streets and insist on sneaking a soft warmth into my heart. I thaw with their melted-chocolate voices. I feel such love for everyone I pass that I smile and nod, and say, "Merry Christmas!" to folks who just stare at me with confused expressions over their Christmas lists and screaming children.

When I pass an open church door, I go inside and listen to the choir. The buskers on the streets receive the rest of my change, and I stop to watch the people who are watching. Two old ladies dance and sing along to a marimba player's rendition of 'Brown Girl in the Ring'. Two children, drunk on holiday spirit, hold each other by the hands and spin around – faster and faster – to the sound of a bell orchestra playing 'God Rest Ye Merry Gentlemen'.

Christmas in the city means heartache, heartache, heartache. A man sleeps in the doorway of what used to be a sandwich shop, and he looks so cold that I give him my coffee. I blush when he rejects it and asks for change instead. Since I gave my change to the buskers, I offer him a trip to McDonalds as compensation, but again, he politely declines.

"Got to keep my health," he says, biting absent-mindedly on a grimy fingernail, "'s all I got, you know?"

At Tesco, I fill the food-bank basket with as many boxes of cereal and biscuits as I can afford. I wrap another box of Fox's Extra Special for your aunt, thinking I'll send it to her anonymously. I wonder if you kept up that tradition after we broke up, or if she's now left to buy her own biscuits. I give it to the homeless man instead, and a card with a twenty-pound note inside.

Winter in the city means changes, changes, changes. Filled with courage, I buy another notebook and pour it full of plans for the new year. I sign up for a gym and give myself a manicure for Christmas. I buy a dress two sizes too small, thinking it will be my goal dress, something to work for, to aim at, to notice. I buy a German course on my credit card and book a trip to Berlin in July. 2018 will be the year, I just feel it in my fingers.

Then I watch *Love Actually* and *The Holiday* twice each, but it's not until I catch the end of *Elf* that I realise this has all been in vain. All these things I don't need are now cluttering up my room. The gym membership I won't use is mocking me from the table, and the notebook I won't ever touch again lies balanced on top of eleven other notebooks marking new starts and other projects. It's the quiet after the end credits. The gap between the Christmas songs and the lack of hot chocolate in my mouth. That's when I feel it. That I miss you the most this time of year. I sigh. A deep and proper sigh from somewhere deep and sore.

And then I text you 'Merry Christmas!' and smile when you text back.

Christmas in the city means miss you, miss you, miss you. It doesn't mean I want you back, or that I regret decisions we made back then. It just means that at Christmas, when the city's full of people and they run around with glitter in their eyes, I want to go back to who we were, with chestnuts roasting on an open fire and the hope of a white Christmas still intact.

I put on my coat, my scarf and my mittens, and walk to a bar down the street. We're a throng now, around Christmas, we who miss who we used to be, and we toast each other with tear-streaked faces, warpaint of city dust and hopes for the future. We toast and sing along to the radio, and *know* with a certainty made of concrete and steel, that next year – next Christmas – we will be somewhere else completely.

Christmas in the city means hoping, hoping, hoping. So I hope, and walk, and the city is there. Always changing, and always the same, carrying me forward, knowing my name.

How Adrian Clarke almost ruined Christmas

Mrs. Mitchell had often thought that ageing seemed to be a slow process of drying up. It was as if every single part of her had lost the moisture keeping it full and firm, and was left stringy, saggy or crispy. It surprised her, therefore, to notice that her hands – for the first time in at least a decade – were clammy against the piano keys.

She smiled at people as they entered the church and sank down into the wooden pews. She had nodded at old students and shaken hands with the elders, acting as

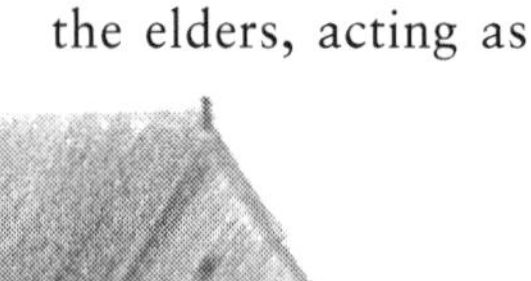

if everything was just as it should be. A large part of her mind, however, was thinking that today would have been a very good day for a small fire in the church. Not a *serious* fire, mind you. She wouldn't want anything to get permanently damaged. But a small electrical fire, perhaps. Just enough smoke that they'd need to cancel the service, but easy enough to fix as soon as the fire marshal had taken a look.

This level of stress was not like her. She blamed eight-year-old Adrian Clarke. She felt sorry for his parents, she really did. Despite his young age, he had crept into her life and brought such chaos and turmoil that she – for one – felt certain he would have been better off in some institution or another. He never stopped asking questions, he didn't have much respect for tradition, and worst of all, he was obnoxiously charming to those with weak minds. Too many of which, she had found, were part of their congregation.

She found it most peculiar. Everyone else seemed to be a little enamoured with the young boy. Even Father Jonas, who – despite his young age, bleeding heart and unbecoming love for modernisation – she found a relatively sensible man, had laughed and said, "What about that Clarke kid, 'ey? He's somethin' else, in'ee?" There hadn't been a single mention of exorcism or child-protective services, and it irked her something fierce.

To her, Adrian Clarke had been nothing but trouble from the moment he'd appeared in November. His family had just moved to the village, and he had wanted to be in the nativity play with the other children. Despite her numerous suggestions, there was no screening process in place for Sunday school and so, Adrian Clarke had been welcomed in.

Mrs. Mitchell had been in charge of the church nativity

for well over 30 years. She had never had problems before. Younger children would have watched the nativity growing up and received instructions from their older siblings, if they had any. The older siblings, in turn, would have gotten instructions from their parents – most of which had been in the play themselves when they were young. The nativity was the same every year. There had been no need to change it.

It was simple setup. Father Andrews, bless his soul, and later, Father Jonas, would read the Christmas story at the front of the church. She would play 'Silent Night' on the piano as accompaniment. The prettiest girl and the eldest boy would walk up the aisle as Mary and Joseph, and the innkeeper would meet them halfway and turn them away from his inn. With sad faces, Mary and Joseph would walk to the altar, where – their backs turned to the audience – Mary's pillow would be replaced by a lovely baby doll. It would lie serenely in the manger made of milk crates, and remind them all what Christmas was *really* about.

Whichever girl had the prettiest hair would play the angel of the Lord and appear to the shepherds. The three most sensible boys would play the Magi, carrying her jewelery box, a carafe she'd inherited from her grand aunt Petunia and a silver napkin holder as gifts for baby Jesus. Any additional girls would play angels, any additional boys would play shepherds and sheep. It was simple, it was beautiful, and *everyone* knew it this way.

From his very first session, Adrian Clarke had caused trouble.

"Hold on a minute," Adrian Clarke had said. Mrs. Mitchell had just started reading the Christmas story, passing out roles as they appeared. She hadn't even made it to the innkeeper before the boy piped up.

"No, excuse *me*," he said, drawing the last vowel until she couldn't ignore his question, "what do you mean there was *no* room for them? How much space do you need to let a lady lie down, *really*?" Then, before she had time to consider his question, he jumped from his chair and lay down on the floor with his arms glued to his side like a tin soldier.

"Look," he said, "It's hardly any room at all. Are you saying that there wasn't a *single* space left on the floor, anywhere? That makes no sense."

"There was no *guest* room left for them," Mrs. Mitchell explained. "All the hotels were full."

"Didn't anyone have a living room or a sofa or something?"

"I suppose not, because so many people were traveling there. They were all full," she said, then tried to continue. "Now..."

"No, *hold on*, hold on, hold on," Adrian said, sitting back up and waving his hand at her. "You're not even allowed to *sit* on the tube if a pregnant woman comes in, you absolutely *must* give her your seat," he said. Adrian had come from London, a mystical, magical place for the other children in the group – who were now nodding with serious faces, proving that they, too, knew that pregnant ladies were to be seated whenever possible. "I'm fairly sure you're not supposed to let them *give birth*," another underlining hand gesture, "in *stables*." He'd pushed his round glasses back onto his freckled nose and peered at her for explanation.

"Well, that's how it was back then," she said, clearing her throat. She insisted they'd all need to raise their hands if they wanted to ask a question, then carried on reading.

She ignored the close-to-levitating Adrian Clarke. She didn't care if he forced his shoulder out of its socket, the way he pushed his hand higher and higher into the air. She carried on, and they made it all the way to the shepherds in the fields without interruption. She assigned the roles to the two Johnsons' boys and the youngest son of Constable Smith.

"I want to be a shepherd too!" Emilia Smith said.

"No dear, you'll be an angel," Mrs. Mitchell smiled.

"I don't want to be no stupid angel!" Emilia said. "I want to be a shepherd! With a cane!"

"You can't be a shepherd, the boys are shepherds. The shepherds are always boys," Mrs. Mitchell snapped, her patience wearing a little thin around the edges.

She could still have kept order if she had just pressed on at that moment, she knew, but Adrian would have flown off his seat if she didn't acknowledge him soon, and she needed to distract Emilia Smith, whose lip was quivering in the most disconcerting manner.

"Yes, Adrian?" Mrs. Mitchell said.

"I don't see why Emilia can't be a shepherd?" he said, pinching his chin as if pondering. "How do you know they were *all* boys? There may have been *some* girls, sometimes? If one of them got sick or something?"

"I think they were all men," she said.

"Well," he said, looking around for support. "If we are going to make it how it *really* was," he continued, with a voice Mrs. Mitchell had known she'd learn to loathe, "wouldn't the innkeeper be an adult, though? And Joseph and Mary too? Adelaide is only 9, actually, I don't think she *can* get pregnant, do you?" He sniffed. "Maybe our parents should do the play instead?" A murmur of approval spilled out from the other kids. Mrs. Mitchell sighed.

"Well, we need more angels, so everyone can't be a shepherd."

"I'd like to be an angel, Miss," Dylan Fredericks said.

"But you're going to be one of the Magi," she said, taken aback by her most loyal and trustworthy Magi wanting to pass on the chance to carry her jewelry box around.

"I'm *always* a Magi though," he said, "I'd like to be an angel this time, please, if you don't mind."

"I'll be the Magi instead of you!" Suzie Jones said. "You can swap with me!" And before Mrs. Mitchell could do anything about it, the children were passing out the roles among themselves, trading positions and making deals.

"You can be Mary this year," Adelaide Montague said to one of the Forester twins, "but then I want to be the innkeeper next year, okay?"

It took Mrs. Mitchell several minutes to calm them down, and she had abandoned any hope of keeping the roles filled the way she wanted them.

"Are we *quite* finished?" she said at last, her voice shaking with indignant fury.

"Mrs. Mitchell?" said Adrian Clarke, whose strong suit was not reading the mood of the room. "I think I'd like to be the narrator, please."

She blinked. "The narrator?" she said, confused.

"Yeah, you know, the one who's doing the voiceover. Telling the story," he clarified, as she still looked like she didn't understand him.

"No, absolutely not. Father Jonas will read the story," she said.

"Why?"

"It's tradition, and he likes to do it," she snapped.

"But I don't have a role," he said. An unchristian spark flared up in her heart as she realised she could make him a sheep, but just as she was about to shut down this line of conversation, there was a knock on the door. Father Jonas stepped in, smiling, as always.

"How are we doing in here?" he said.

"Father Jonas, please, sir," Adrian said, bowing his head deeply as if greeting a royal. "Would you mind if I was the narrator this year? I'm a *very* good reader," he added, as if giving his credentials.

"That's a great idea!" Father Jonas said, clapping his hands. Mrs. Mitchell could see, then, in the gleam running through the eyes of the children, and the wink Father Jonas gave Adrian Clarke when he thought she couldn't see them, that she had a full-blown mutiny on her hands.

"Fine," she said. "But now we need to get focused!"

And that had been that, she'd thought. But rehearsals hadn't gone the way she wanted them to. The kids had been whispering, meeting in corners. She'd always felt there was something going on right behind her back. And nothing could just *be* the way it was supposed to be without discussion. Adrian Clarke had argued that the gifts of the Magi were not safe to give a child. He argued that baby Jesus would put a piece of gold in his mouth and choke to death.

"And then what about the salvation of all sinners?" he had said, waving his hands at her as if she, personally, had been the one to suggest these inappropriate gifts. "We'd all be *screwed*," he'd added, earning himself a time-out in the costume corner. But the discussion hadn't ended just because his back was turned to them, oh no! Myrrh, he explained, was no better, as children were supposed to have products for sensitive skin.

"I'd bring him a teddy bear, or something," he said.

"Or some clothes. Babies need a lot of clothes," said Suzie Jones, who had just gotten a baby brother herself.

Not even the shepherds went clear of scrutiny. A big discussion had broken out over why the shepherds trusted an angel who was just *telling* them not to be afraid. They all knew that someone just saying "you can trust me" wasn't enough. Mrs. Mitchell had to bring out her sternest retired-teacher voice to make them realise that it would, in fact, *not* make more sense for the shepherds to go and notify the police, and say that someone claiming to be an angel had tried to get them to follow them into a dark stable.

"But it's not like they knew it was an angel," Adrian said, "and there could have been nothing in there but a goat and a cow and an axe murderer or something."

She really wanted to believe everything was back on track now. The parents were in their pews, the lights were dimmed, and all the children had turned up on time, with their costumes washed and pressed as per instruction. But there was still that flicker of doubt… Something she was missing. One of the Forester twins had come carrying a basket in through the side door. Looking to both sides before running in behind the curtain, as if carrying a secret. Mrs. Mitchell didn't like secrets. There had also been an unexplained top hat in the annex, and most tellingly of all, Adrian Clarke had – up to five minutes ago – been looking pale and nervous. After a whispered word with Suzie Jones, he had grinned, and now he looked fine. The kids were up to something. She knew it now. With seconds left to start, the certainty was overwhelming. The kids were up to something.

But it was time. She looked at Father Jonas, who nodded at her. Taking a deep breath to calm her nerves, she started playing. Adrian Clarke came out between the curtains and grinned.

"In those days..." he began, opening his Bible, "Caesar Augustus issued a decree that a census should be taken of the entire Roman world." So far so good. Joseph – this year played by chubby little Yu Kwan – and Mary, a Forester twin, walked up the aisle. Mary looked about ready to burst with a holy baby and had a severe waddle, taught to her by Suzie Jones. They made their way up the aisle, stopped halfway to knock on a door, and the other Forester twin opened. Adrian stopped reading.

"Yes?" the Forester twin rumbled, her face partially obscured by a wash mop acting as beard. Mrs. Mitchell stiffened. There were *not* supposed to be lines.

"My name's Joseph, and I'm going to marry this woman, 'cause she's promised me, but as you can see, she's a bit pregnant, and we really need a space to sleep," said Yu. "She's small," he added, "she won't take up much space at all." The adults shifted in their seats, a low murmur and some laughter washed through the room, some shot glances at Mrs. Mitchell. Some of them had been in on it, she realised. A full-blown mutiny indeed.

"I'm really sorry," the innkeeper boomed, "I've got people on every single square inch of my entire house. You won't *believe* how many people have come to write their name into this census thingy," she said, wiping her forehead as if to show just how much of a strain this historical event had been.

"Can't one of them give up their place for a pregnant lady? I'll happily sleep outside, but she's really rather pregnant," Joseph begged. The innkeeper scratched her curly beard.

"I tell you what," she said, in the haggling voice of her father, the car salesman. "I've got this stable you can use. It's actually better than sleeping inside, as there are no other people there, only some animals, who are very nice. Here," she said, reaching behind the door and handing them a basket. "Here's some food and some blankets so you won't be too uncomfortable. One should always be nice to pregnant ladies," she added. "Good night!"

Mrs. Mitchell felt dizzy, and put all her energy into repeating 'Silent Night' over and over. Mary and Joseph were making themselves comfortable near the altar, and Adrian Clarke continued.

"While they were there, the time came for the baby to be born, and she gave birth to her firstborn, a son."

Mary suddenly screamed as if a dozen demons were running through her body. The entire church seemed to jump on its foundation, startled by the unexpected sound.

"It hurt a lot, because when Eve ate the apple in the garden of Eden, God said women should give birth in pain, and this was like, the holiest baby, so it probably hurt a little extra," Adrian Clarke shouted above the noise of Mary's birth.

"Push!" Joseph called as Mary screamed. "Push!" he called, with all the power of a football player used to shouting directions from the sidelines. From under Mary's robe came a crying – nay, screaming – abomination that made Mrs. Mitchell stop playing for a full two seconds in pure shock. The crowd gasped.

"Babies are gross when they're born," Adrian Clarke explained, "and Mary hadn't had one before, so she was probably be a bit scared."

"Ewwwww," Mary said dramatically, holding the baby up by its leg. "It's disgusting, and scary!" It was, in fact, just a baby doll. The crying kind. It was covered in ketchup or theatre blood, and had yellow bits – chicken salad? – smeared here and there for effect.

"But Mary cleaned it, wrapped it in cloths and put it in a manger, because that was the very best place they could find in the stable, and they wanted the baby to be safe and comfortable." The familiar Christmas scene settled as soon as the baby doll stopped crying.

"There were shepherds living out on the fields nearby, keeping watch over their flocks at night," said Adrian. The shepherds were shielding their eyes with their hands, seemingly scouting for sheep this way and that.

"An angel of the Lord appeared to them," said Adrian, and a big CRACK rattled the pews again. A cloud of smoke sprung from the floor, and Dylan Fredericks – who was very into magic tricks – jumped out into the wafting centre. The shepherds screamed and scrambled out of the way, terrified.

"DON'T BE SCARED!" the angel shouted. "I am the great ANGEL OF THE LORD and I have come to bring you GOOD NEWS!" He shook his arm, and a big bouquet of plastic flowers sprung to life.

"TODAY, in the town of David," the angel continued, whipping a top hat out from behind his wings, "a SAVIOUR HAS BEEN BORN!" he yelled, dragging a little toy rabbit out of the hat. "GO AND LOOK!"

"We will! Because now that we see you are magical, we know we can trust you!" said one of the shepherds, suddenly at ease with this new visitor.

"Good!" The angel said, then went on to give them clear and concise directions to the baby, and sent them on their way. The remaining angels gathered on stage, and as a complete surprise to Mrs. Mitchell and the audience alike, they sang.

Glory to God in the highest heaven,
And on Earth, peace to those on whom his favour rests.

The melody was simple. A few prolonged vowels, and some ups and downs. It bore resemblance to old medieval chants, thought Mrs. Mitchell. But with the tender children's voices, it had a fragile beauty to it that crept in through your head and into your heart. They sang the song over and over, and Mrs. Mitchell stopped playing the piano all together. As they sang, the children lit the paper lantern strung up over the heads of Joseph and Mary. A big warm star. The shepherds wandered up to them and put down plush sheep by their feet. Plush sheep, Mrs. Mitchell thought, that she had expressly forbidden.

"And Magi came from somewhere in the far east, probably China, but no one knows," Adrian continued over the singing, "and they'd been asked by Herod to go find the holy baby and tell him where it was. He wanted to kill it, but he pretended that he just wanted to worship it. But the Magi had a weird dream – I don't know if all of them did or just the one," he added, as an afterthought to himself, "but they dreamed they shouldn't go back to King Herod, so they just went to the baby, gave him their presents, and went away."

The Magi, led by Suzie Jones, carried the jewelery box, carafe and silver napkin holder, as planned. But in addition, they came carrying an assortment of teddy bears, baby clothes and a jumbo pack of nappies.

"Thank you so much," said Mary. "We are *very* poor."

"Not anymore!" said one of the Magi. "Gold is worth a lot of money. You can probably buy a house now."

"Thank you!" said Joseph, his voice shaking with emotion. "That's just what I wanted for my wife and child. To keep them safe!" He threw himself around the nearest

Magi's neck in gratitude.

"Glory to God in the highest heaven, and on Earth, peace to those on whom his favour rests," the angels sang, over and over. The Magi bowed to baby Jesus and walked their way down the aisle, shooting worried glances at each other. Something wasn't going to plan. Adrian Clarke waved, trying to catch Mrs. Mitchell's attention.

"You have to keep playing," he hissed. "We need a new verse." She nodded, played another round of 'Silent Night', and noticed that the kids stopped singing their own song right before the end of the verse.

"Silent night," they sang, "holy night…" Then Adrian Clarke flapped his hands to make everyone join in.

"Everybody!" he called.

"All is calm, all is bright," they all sang. Smiling parents, adoring elders, and even Father Jonas, who had tears in his eyes.

Round yon virgin, mother and child,
Holy infant so tender and mild,
Sleep in heavenly peace,
Sleep in heavenly peace.

The last tone died out, leaving the church quiet and expectant. Mary accidentally kicked the manger a little, making baby Jesus cry. The room held its breath as the curtain-clad Mary lifted baby Jesus up, cradled him in her arms, and rocked him until the doll fell quiet.

"Merry Christmas!" called Adrian Clarke. And Mrs. Mitchell began the applause.

How we (don't) celebrate Christmas

This is our home. This door, with the chipped blue paint and the shadows of black mould along the glass. This living room filled with second-hand furniture, worn-down cushions and DVDs from floor to ceiling. The LEGO Death Star hanging in a window and the collectible Batman figurines, these are the knick-knacks we've chosen. The oil paintings by your brother and the silk-screen prints we made in a workshop, the holiday pictures and movie posters on the walls. This is our life in a box, a box with us in it, a box we have built.

Outside, there is Christmas. Thousands of lights costing thousands of pounds, bleeding electricity out from our tax fund, haemorrhaging environmental concerns as every minor D-list celebrity says, "3... 2... 1... ooooooh!" and flips the switches of Everywhere. Outside, people run around in circles, procuring plastic toys for their children's vast collections and useless knick-knacks no one will ever love. Not really.

But not here. We love everything we keep, as a rule. We're not minimalists, not by any stretch of the imagination. But we're fundamentalist creatives with a love of what we love. In here, nothing will change as December draws towards the end. The candles on the table are in their regular holders, and we won't even put a Santa's hat on the cactus like we used to. This is our home.

We don't celebrate Christmas. We bring no glittering tack into our home, we don't keep possessions that can only be put out once a year. We don't buy gifts to anyone. My family has had longer to get used to it, but even yours seem to begrudgingly accept our 'life choices' now. They've also stopped giving us anything, which is good – it keeps us in balance. They don't create an unbalanced debt, nor do we create a false expectation. Instead, we all share presents throughout the year. Spontaneous, heartfelt, 'I saw this and thought of you' gifts. We don't gather them up for a random tree-clad December day. This is better. This is what we do.

There will be no angels lining the shelves, or trips to a church we don't go to the rest of the year. We'll plan no extravagant meal that repeats from year to year. There will be no Brussel sprouts that no one enjoys but everyone eats. Our meal will have no traditions where everyone needs to be quiet at the right time, or sing the same songs with serious faces and fake sincerity. To us, Christmas is just a day like any other. A few days like all the others. But they're days we get together. An extra weekend or a holiday just for us. Days we choose to cherish, although they're just the same.

On Christmas Eve, we'll make mac 'n' cheese and watch *Tomb Rider 1* and 2. We both agree they're pretty bad, but they make us laugh, and we so rarely make time to watch bad movies just for fun. Then we'll open a bottle of port and a big tub of ice cream. Perfect companions to *Charlie's Angels 1* and 2. We'll cheer, sip our drinks and call, "Bosley!" every time a Bosley comes on screen, and you'll curl up against me, and get the thick blanket from the bedroom. Maybe we'll make hot chocolate and add a splash of rum. Perhaps we'll call our parents and my grandma to say merry Christmas, as it's more important to them than to us – and no reason not to, when you get right down to it. It's just a greeting, like any other, but it makes them happy, so of course we will.

On Christmas Day, we'll stay in bed until late, then have some friends over for lunch. They don't celebrate Christmas either, so they always come around to ours. We'll make tapas, perhaps a cake. Nothing too festive, just some nice party food. Then we'll watch all of *The Lord of the Rings* or the original *Star Wars* trilogy, or maybe *Harry Potter* this year. We'll have popcorn and Jonas – who's a bit more traditional than the rest of us – will make mulled cider in the evening. Sometimes, more friends will join us on their way home from family, and they'll bring leftover cookies and cake for the table.

At night, when they've all got home, unless someone is too tired and needs to crash, you'll reveal to me your new underwear – some laced number, I'm sure – and we'll snuggle up in bed and talk about our friends and how lucky we are to have them. These exact ones, what are the odds, that we've found in this bustling city. Then we'll talk about how much nicer it is, this calm and quiet way of hanging out, without strict traditions, or religious or consumerist pressures, or family conflicts for dinner. And we'll nod and agree that we've found the best way to take advantage of these days off, these days that are like all the others.

Perhaps it will snow, and we'll wrap up in our duvet and go to the window. We'll look down at all the lanterns lit in the graveyard and the lights from all the trees. We'll watch as the large flakes drift past our window and marvel at how quiet the city is at Christmas. When you fall asleep, I will watch your face – like I always do – and send a quiet thank-you into the night. A thank-you for getting to share my life with you who feels like I do about Christmas. I'll kiss your nose, and you will stir and cuddle closer to me, and my arms will feel the strongest they ever do as I wrap them around you at the end of the day.

This is our home. This Christmas-less flat full of secular decorations that don't change with the season, only with the years. This is our life in a box with us in it, the smell of mulled cider faintly in the air, popcorn under the couch and a drunk friend on it. This is where you sleep, wrapped in my arms, and I smile, loving you deeply.

We don't celebrate Christmas, I don't think we ever will. But still, it's my favourite time of year.

The magical shop that was suddenly there

If anyone in town thought about it all, they would probably swear the shop had never been there before. It stood right between the café where the rude fella used to work and that designer store with the beautiful shoes. The building itself was a bit shorter than the neighbouring two, of a different type of brick completely. But the pavement outside ran smoothly and uninterrupted, the way you'd expect, and with every cracked tile in its perfect place. That alone was enough for no one to think about it. Everyone in town knew that buildings didn't simply appear overnight.

But you and I, just between us, we know that there is more between heaven and earth. And one of those things is this unexpected shop of perfect Christmas presents.

The shopkeeper's name was Liam. He opened his eyes and looked out the window. Spotting the cathedral down the road, he nodded to himself. *It must be December eighth*, he thought, and that was all he needed before opening the shop. He turned on the tiny lights on the Christmas tree in the window. He switched on the record player and carefully swung the needle down at 'The Christmas Song'. He hummed along, sometimes singing the harmonies, while unpacking a large crate by the wall.

The crate held the strangest things. With a gentle touch, he placed an antique chess board on the shelf, aligning each piece in its proper place. A small plastic monkey got a place on the table by the door, and a large woollen scarf was tied around the neck of the shop's only mannequin.

"There you go," he smiled, brushing the scarf smooth, "you look smashing!"

There was a keyring that would respond with an optimistic 'BEEP BEEP!' if you whistled for it, and a necklace with a two-piece heart stating 'BEST 4' on one half and 'FRIENDS EVER' on the other. He wrinkled his nose when pulling out a large ceramic cookie jar in the shape of a pineapple. It was painted in garish pink, and sprinkled with glitter and rhinestones.

"Oh dear," he said, "I don't dare to think who's waiting for you."

Although the crate was large, it could have worried the casual observer to see the man filling his entire shop from a single box no larger than a big suitcase. However, no casual observer was present this early in the morning, and if one had been, they'd probably not have noticed. People rarely do.

Soon, the shop was filled with the most beautiful items, all placed and stacked in neat rows and columns. Each of them had a grey manila tag tied to it, each of them declaring the price to be £4.99.

"Right," Liam said, brushing his hand through his thick black beard, "I wonder if there will be..." he said to himself, stepping through a curtain in the back and opening a small cupboard to his left.

"Perfect!" he said, fishing out a croissant, a cafetiere, a mismatched mug and plate, and a small kettle.

"Coffee," he mumbled, "Coffee, coffee... here we are. My favourite!" he said, finding the Ethiopian dark roast on the table.

He ate his breakfast slowly, watching people pass by on the street outside. Every now and then, someone would stop, scowl and the shop, then shrug and hurry on. Other times, old ladies would pass. They would eye the shop suspiciously, shudder and shake their heads. One of them even crossed herself, more certain in her ways than younger folks. But Liam didn't mind. They'd find out soon enough, and he was in no hurry. Everyone who entered here would leave happier than they'd arrived, and although his ways may be unorthodox, he hardly felt he could be accused of evil. Pleasing people was the whole point, wasn't it?

He yawned. The mornings were always the worst. The special magic of the shop took some time to leak out into the town, and not before it had saturated the streets completely would people begin to show up.

The door rang.

"Excuse me," said a young girl with a serious face.

"Yes?" Liam smiled and brushed the crumbs out of his beard. "How can I help you, young lady?"

"It says on the door that you have the perfect Christmas present for *anyone*," she said, eyeing him with a look much older than her years.

"That's right!" Liam said. "Just tell me who you're shopping for, and I'll help you find the gift."

"The *perfect* gift?" the girl said.

Liam scoffed and made a dismissive gesture. "That goes without saying. The perfect gift."

She rubbed her nose a couple of times, meeting his eyes the whole time. "Okay," she said, as if he'd passed some great test, "I need a Christmas present for my grandpa. He's..."

"No, no, don't tell me," Liam said, looking around. "Just answer a couple of questions, okay?" The girl nodded.

"What does he talk about the most?"

The girl thought about it, wringing her face with effort. "Granny," she said, punctuating her statement with a firm nod.

"I see. Is she alive?" Liam said. The girl shook her head. "What does he smell like?" he asked. He was walking around the shop with long steps, stopping occasionally to move things around on the shelves. The question didn't appear odd to the girl. She just closed her eyes and took a deep breath through her nose.

"Like yucky candy he keeps in his pocket, and like the type of cream that stings on your skin, and like chicken poo and potatoes," she said, opening her eyes and looking at him expectantly.

"I see," Liam nodded, twisting the ends of his beard between his fingers, "and what is the word of his heart?" he said.

"What's that?"

"The word that he says more than other people say it. The word that he can't stop using, even though it's just a word. It can be a nice word or a bad word, it doesn't matter, just the word that you'd say 'that's my grandpa's word' about, you see?"

"Hm..." said the girl, pinching her chin a couple of times, thinking. "Oh! I know! It's 'nonsense'," she said. "He always says that. This is nonsense, or that nonsense with the Prime Minister, or the nonsense we're having for dinner. He says it *all the time*."

"Right," Liam said. He stopped in front of one of the low benches and picked up a worn deck of cards with drawings of ladies in sailor's outfits on. "Here you go. He'll love these. Especially if you play with him."

Her eyes widened. "He's got two ladies just like that on his arms!" she said, grinning. "That's *perfect*!" Then her face dropped a little. "It looks very old... is it awfully expensive?"

"It's £4.99," said Liam. The girl gave a big grin and handed him a bunched-up £5 note.

"Here's your penny," he said and pointed to a little clay well by the till. "You can get a wish for it if you want. Just close your eyes, make a wish, and give your penny to the well. But you can't tell anyone your wish," Liam said seriously. "Then it won't come true."

"Thank you very much!" the girl said after having bought her wish. Liam smiled and she disappeared out the door.

A few minutes later, two young boys entered.

"Good morning, boys," said Liam. "You off to school?" They looked at him, rolled their eyes, mumbled a reply. They walked around the shop, looking at things and laughing at them. Offhand remarks about how tacky and garish everything was. Liam smiled in his beard, wondering what was waiting for them in here. They were good mates, he could tell. They were only 12 or 13, and they both presented cool-guy masks that hadn't yet been worn smooth with experience. And yet, they seemed relaxed around each other. Their way of interacting was old. Honest. A rare quality, in Liam's experience.

The tallest of the two gasped like a heroine in an old movie.

"It's... I... I had the exact same one..." he said, picking up a blue teddy bear with a green bow. He looked at it as if he couldn't quite believe his eyes. "Before the fire... It was my favourite," he said. "Mine even had a few stitches on the ear just like this one... It looks just like Mister Caramel..." He blushed a little. His face revealed a hectic attempt at finding a joke or a way out of this sudden onset of emotion, but instead he dragged the back of his sleeve across his face. His mate put an arm around his shoulders.

"Do you want it?" he said. "It can be your Christmas present."

The first boy nodded, knocked his head gently against his friend's, and sniffed. His mate held out his hand to take the teddy to the till, but the taller boy was reluctant to let it go and just walked up with him.

"How much is it?"

"That depends," said Liam. "Would you like a wish each from the wishing well?"

The boys looked at each other. "Whatever," the shorter one said, and shrugged.

"Then it's £4.98," said Liam. "Gives you a wish each."

When the boys turned to leave, the tallest had a new Mister Caramel in his backpack, and both had slipped their pennies into the wishing well with just the right amount of aloof lack of interest not to get embarrassed and just enough sincere respect not to jinx themselves.

A suit-clad man came running in through the door just as the boys left.

"Listen," he said, heading straight for the till, "I need a Christmas present for... that's *perfect*," he said, picking up the beeping keyring. "She's always losing her keys." He hurried to pay the £4.99 and started heading out the door before he had gotten his change.

"Your penny!" Liam called, "You can get a wish if you want one!"

The man stopped for a split second, looked back at the wishing well. "You have it, mate! Enjoy your day," and then he was off.

Liam looked at the penny. He wondered if the man understood the colossal opportunity he had passed up, or how big a gift he had given to this stranger in the shop. The penny felt heavy in his hand. What should he wish for? He quite liked his life in the shop of perfect gifts.

I'd like some company, he thought, then dropped the penny in the well. It was a simple wish, and he felt it came through mere moments later, when an old lady came in through the door and spent a full hour telling him about her husband before realising the antique chess set would be *perfect*.

The rest of the day passed quickly. People came and went, and by eight o'clock, every single item in the shop had been picked up except the pink pineapple with glitter and rhinestones, and the green scarf on the mannequin. Two young women came through the door.

"You closed?" they said, gasping for air. "We've heard you have great stuff, and we…" then they both noticed the pink pineapple and started howling with laughter.

"Oh, my god, that's *perfect*!" one of them screamed, "she's going to love it!"

"It's as if it was made for her," the other one gasped, and they were both so into their own enjoyment of the pineapple that Liam couldn't get any sensible information out of them about this person who'd love a pink pineapple cookie jar. He sighed.

It was three past eight. Usually, the store would be closing by now, but the scarf was still there. It worried him a little. He had never been left with items before, and he didn't know what to do. He wondered if he should try putting it back in the crate, or just leave it and see if it turned up again tomorrow. He went back into the little kitchen and made himself another coffee. Then he sat down in the store to wait. It was quarter past eight, half past, quarter to nine, nine forty-five, ten fifteen. He sighed again.

Just as he stood up to start closing, the door rang.

"Hey!" said the girl in the long purple coat. Under her arm was the pink pineapple.

"Hello," Liam said, smiling. "I take it it wasn't perfect," he said, nodding to the cookie jar. The woman laughed. She had short dark hair and a smile so charming that Liam wished he wasn't going to be somewhere else completely tomorrow morning.

"Not really," she grinned. "What else have you got?"

"This scarf must be yours," he said, lifting it off the mannequin and draping it around her neck. She smelled faintly of apricots, he thought, and cinnamon, almonds and dew. He swallowed. Her skin felt warm against his fingers.

"No, I *don't* think so," she said, wrinkling her nose.

"Oh..." Liam said, looking around. "That's all I've got, I'm afraid..."

"Actually," she said, rummaging around in her coat pockets, "do you have a job for me?" She pulled out a dishevelled CV, a handful of curled-up paper and ink. "I'm happy to do anything, I'm good with people and I make a mean cup of tea," she said.

"I... this shop doesn't really... I don't think..." Liam said, but found himself distracted by the way her eyes laughed with the light of the Christmas tree and the way the scarf lay against her neck.

"I'm happy to travel," she said. "I know this is a pop-up shop. I'll come with you!"

"But..." Liam said, then sighed. "What's your name?"

"Company," she said, rolling her eyes. "My parents were hippies."

"Really?" Liam stuttered, and as she began telling their story, he fell down into a world where time passed in new and unexpected ways. At eleven o'clock, he laughed as she told him about a play she had written. It had been a *serious play*, she explained, about umbrellas falling in love but only seeing each other when it rained. At one thirty, he found himself telling her the story of how he came to run this store. He told her about the Christmas where he had been out of all options, and saw no solution in sight. He told her about the old woman who had run the store and wished for a new recruit, and how he'd loved it from the very first second. A few minutes past three, she admitted that she had moved around her whole life and only now begun missing having somewhere to call home. And at four twenty-five, she threw the green scarf around his neck and pulled him so close he could smell the apricot almond dew on her lips.

"No, I think you're right," she said, "this scarf is perfect..." and then she kissed him, and he kissed her back.

At five fifty-five, the earth shifted beneath their feet as the shop closed and moved to Bristol, where it would open between a bookshop specialising in travel books and a grubby little lane, and no one would be any the wiser. At nine forty, they woke up from their slumber in a big armchair in the back. Company went to a shop nearby and bought them croissants, coffee and enough biscuits to fill the pineapple to the brim. When she came back, she hung the green scarf by the door and watched as Liam started unpacking the crate of the day. She leaned against the door and sighed with delight.

Yes, she thought to herself. *This is perfect.*

The nisse of Granvik Farm

With his red knitted hat and traditional clothing, the Norwegian nisse looks like something out of a Christmas legend. Perhaps that's why we now only pull him out for Christmas decorations, songs and stories. We call Father Christmas a nisse too, just to add to the confusion. But the nisse, as a matter of fact, is there all year round, living in the barn and keeping the farm safe.

Everyone used to know you should treat your nisse right. Otherwise, his pranks could be mischievous or even turn cruel, if your deeds were particularly dark. He would tie knots in your horse's mane, turn your cow's milk sour, and some say he could even bring disease to your family if you offended him deeply enough. If you were kind to your nisse, however, he'd help take care of your animals; keep them healthy, happy and well-groomed. At Christmas, you'd thank him for another year's friendship by leaving out a bowl of rice porridge for him. Maybe even a bottle of beer if you had one to spare, or a cup of fresh milk if you didn't.

But this was in the good old days. Children still sing about him, sure, but they keep confusing him with Father Christmas and expecting presents in return for their porridge, if they put out anything at all. Most people don't. They've replaced the tradition with a fireside helping of cookies and milk, starving the poor creature in the barn completely.

The nisse at Granvik Farm hadn't seen a single grain of rice for a generation and a half. And he understood, now, that all the power he'd once thought he had was a lie dependent on livestock. The barn was silent except for the rattling of mice. There hadn't been animals in here for so long, he'd started to forget what it felt like – leaning his cheek against a friendly cow or braiding the tail of a horse. But the quiet was the worst. Sometimes, he thought he hadn't had a proper night's sleep since the last animals left, 30 years ago. The cold and quiet would push against him all night and keep him from finding rest. It simply wasn't right, he thought. A barn should be a place of noise and warmth and life and smells. Not this mausoleum of the way things used to be.

It was nearing Christmas now. He could tell because of the hunger that always came sneaking up on him this time of year. This year would be even worse, he thought, since the young farmer and his wife had decided to exchange Christmas trees and Christmas sheaves for sun-tan lotion and margaritas. They hadn't even put lights on the farmyard tree. This, in particular, bothered the nisse. The farm's position had made the Christmas lights visible all the way from town. For years and years, it had been the pride of this little village. It might be a terrible year, but as long as the lights shone at Granvik Farm, everything would be all right. But now, the farm was left in darkness, as if no one cared for it at all.

He wished he could leave, he really did. But the rules were clear: every farm needs a nisse, and as long as the barn was standing, he would live in it. He had, once or twice, toyed with the idea of burning the whole place to the ground, leaving this place behind and finding a farm where there were still animals in the barn. He longed to smell fresh milk and cow dung again. His heart fluttered with the thought of seeing calves in spring or petting the soft muzzle of a horse. But he knew, deep in his heart, that as much as he wanted to, he couldn't harm the barn. He knew this the way he knew that he couldn't breathe underwater or fly in the air. It wasn't in his powers as a nisse. And still – although barely – the love he felt for the farm was stronger than the resentment he felt over the way it was run. This would pass soon, though, he knew. There wasn't much love left at all.

It was snowing now. The cold crept through the cracks in the woodwork and made his knobbly old hands stiff and pale. He had wrapped up in an old horse blanket, and it dawned on him that it had been a couple of days since he last moved. Not good. He needed to keep his blood flowing, after all. Perhaps he should do his little round of the barn, check for broken glass or new mouse nests in the walls. Or maybe he should see if he could find some old grain in the bottom of a sack somewhere, and put it out for the birds. He knew the last of the grain had been put out years ago, but to make himself stand, he decided it was best to be sure.

Moving was a slow process. Not only because he had to soften his cold and stiff muscles in order to stand up, but also because his willpower was just not what it used to be. Come on now, he thought to himself, and then repeated it out loud, just to make sure he'd pay attention. That's when he heard it. Or noticed it, to be more precise. The sound had been there for a while, but hadn't quite made its way into his consciousness, as it was one so unexpected that he hadn't thought it could be true. There were footsteps in the barn. Someone was walking around in here. And soon, they'd find him, if he didn't move out of the way.

Many a farmer has seen the nisse. Their existence is not a secret, per sé, but those who have come upon him have usually done so as a result of months and months of work in the barn. The inevitability of two people working in the same building sooner or later crossing paths.

But the nisse is shy and doesn't want to be seen, so he will usually scuttle away if he hears you coming. The nisse at Granvik Farm, however, knew he had caught on too late. Instead of hiding, he sat very, very still. He knew that for the average human, the idea that he couldn't possibly be there was enough for them to think he wasn't. They'd overrule their own eyes if they knew what they saw couldn't be true. The steps were close now, and he could hear they were accompanied by heavy, gurgling breathing. Someone was walking in the barn who should probably not be walking at all.

The nisse isn't very good with faces. To him, we all look more or less the same. But when old farmer Granvik himself walked into the room, the familiar gait sparked such a feeling of recognition in the old fae's heart that it brought tears to his eyes and a warmth spread through his creaking joints.

The old man slumped down on the edge of a trough and leaned heavily on his cane. He was peering around the room, his eyes half in the present, half back in the days when this room would have been bustling with the sounds of hungry pigs. It pained him to see it like this.

The layer of dust so thick there were grooves along the floor where the mice had run. He'd never expected his son to run the farm, not really, but he had thought – or maybe hoped – that at the very least, he'd keep it all in order. These rooms and these buildings that had meant so much to his family for generations.

He looked at the nisse for a long time before he realised what he was looking at. But when he did, he nodded to himself and tipped his hat in greeting.

"Evenin'," he said. "So you're still hangin' on in here, then?"

The nisse cleared his throat. It had been a long while since he'd spoken to anyone, and when he finally managed to answer, his voice was a shrill squeak compared with what it used to be.

"Aye, and you too?" he said.

The old man nodded again. "Barely, barely," he grumbled. Neither of them spoke for a while.

The nisse noted how this farmer who had once carried hundred-kilo bags of grain over his shoulder was now a dried husk of a man. The farmer, on his side, wondered if it was bitterness that had drawn such deep ridges on the nisse's face.

"Can't be much for you to do out here these days?" he said, picking absentmindedly at a rusty nail in the trough.

The nisse shrugged. "Windows and mice, mostly," he said. Again, the quiet stretched through several minutes. This time, it was the nisse who found a question flickering in his mind. "How come you're not in Thailand, then?"

The old man scoffed. "'S nowhere to celebrate Christmas," he said. "They don't even have pine trees down that way."

"Are you here to look after the house?" asked the nisse.

The old man sighed heavily. "I've moved back in, I'm

afraid. They no longer trust me to take care of my flat, so they've put me up in the annex, where they can keep an eye on me. And vacuum my floors whenever they want," he added with a scowl.

This time, the nisse scoffed, dragging his hand through the layer of dust on the floor next to him. "Right," he said, and left it at that.

The old man stood up after a while. "I best get back in before the cold takes me," he said.

The nisse swallowed and forced himself upright, too. "Yes, and I've got things to do," he said. "Can't just dawdle around all day." Both nodded at each other, touched their hats, then stepped into their evenings as if nothing had happened.

The next day, the nisse found himself doing more chores on the outside of the barn than he had done the past two winters put together. He kept an eye on the main building, half hoping the old man would turn up. Technically, this was breaking the codex of the nisse, placing himself outside like this, increasing the chances of getting spotted. But as far as the nisse was concerned, the codex could go suck an egg. It had been 30 years since he'd had any company that wasn't of the rodent persuasion, and if he could avoid having to wait another 30, he'd do what he could to make it so.

In the early afternoon, he heard the door from the main building slam, and it was all he could do not to turn around and wave to make sure the old farmer noticed him here. He could hear his slow shuffle through the snow, and waited until the steps were right behind him before turning around with feigned surprise.

"Evenin'," the farmer said, seemingly studying the back of his gloved hand. "I see you're keepin' busy?" The nisse pretended to wipe sweat off his forehead, about to say something about having a tremendous amount of stuff to do as the farmer's son did nothing at all. But before he could say anything, the old farmer continued. "Now, we're both busy men, of course, but should you be in want of some company later, I seem to have made a bit too much dinner and wouldn't want to see it go to waste. I can bring you out some to the barn, or..." he said, as if something had suddenly occurred to him, "I'd be happy to share a meal with you if you'd pop around – say, at seven?"

The farmer himself had been taking numerous trips to the window all day, hoping to catch the nisse having a break from his work. When no such diversion from his many tasks had presented itself, he'd decided that Christmas was not a time for silly pride, and gone out to invite him directly. He'd go by the postbox at the same time, so it would look coincidental, of course.

Now, he stood, trying to keep the eagerness from showing on his face, and prepared to hide the disappointment should the nisse reject his invitation.

The nisse's heart leapt. He hadn't been invited into the main house for a good 200 years or so, and as much as he wanted to play it cool, his belly made a rumbling roar at the thought of his first decent meal in 30 years.

Trying to keep a sliver of dignity, he pulled his beard and said, "Could do, could do... I've got quite a lot on my list today so I might be a tad late, but I'll do my best..." And then he did everything he could to let the clock get to five past seven before he knocked on the old wooden door.

Usually, meetings between fae folk and humans fall heavy in awkward conversation, as there's little common ground between them. But for 30-odd years, the old farmer had wanted nothing more than to speak about cattle and crops. And for the same time, not a day had gone by where the nisse had thought of anything else.

If the farmer had been a cook of the modern times, he might have turned the nisse quite ill with avocado toast and coriander, curries, or vegan cheesecake. But the farmer was a simple man. He could boil potatoes to perfection and fry Pollock to within an inch of burning. It was crisp on the outside and stiff all the way through. You wouldn't find it in a restaurant, but he loved it all the same. This was food the way the nisse liked it, too. Simple, greasy and bland.

The following night, they had pork chops and mash, played cards for a while and shared a few drams of scotch. The nisse was small but could hold his liquor, the farmer was old but could do the same. They talked about Asher, the horse the farmer had owned as a young boy.

"He was the best horse," the farmer said, moved by a memory.

"He really was," the nisse said, remembering his equestrian friend with fondness.

December passed and an odd friendship grew. The nisse started sleeping on the bench in the kitchen, the old farmer insisting it was too cold in the barn. Together, they strung Christmas lights on the tree in the farmyard. The farmer went and got bird feeders, milk for rice porridge and a sizable Christmas ham, as well as enough beer and whiskey to last them into the new year.

"I don't think I'll live much longer," the old farmer said as they played poker for his son's money one evening. "Felt it comin' for a while now, the stiffness from within. My last Christmas, that's for sure."

The nisse took a deep swig of his beer. "I'm sorry," he said.

"I'm not!" the farmer burst out in a violent laughter. "I'm relieved, to tell you the truth. This ain't the times for old men. This is a time for young folks and vegetarians. Resilient sorts. Not grumpy ol' buggers like me."

The nisse raised his glass solemnly. "To grumpy ol' buggers!" he said, and they clinked glasses for that through the night.

The nisse told the farmer how he longed for a farm with animals, and how he knew he couldn't get one as long as the barn was standing.

"Don't get me wrong, I love the farm," he hiccuped, getting ready for bed.

"I know you do," said the old man. "I know you do."

On Christmas Eve, the son called from Thailand to wish his father a merry Christmas.

"How are you gettin' on, Pa?" he asked, after telling him all about their snorkeling adventures and the food at the hotel.

"I'm gettin' on all right, son," the old farmer said. "Been puzzling about the old barn, tryin' to get things in order. Lookin' better out there already. May get the old workshop up and runnin' in a day or two," he said, keeping half an eye on the porridge, which was puttering away on the stove.

"Yeah..." the son said, sounding concerned, "about that. Dad... just... don't get too attached, okay? We're considerin' rentin' it out now. This guy Maria knows in the city wants to turn it into storage units for city folks. To keep their furniture and art and that in."

The old man laughed. "Don't they have homes to keep their furniture in?"

"It's for their extra things, Pa," the son said, annoyed. "Just don't get too attached to the barn, yeah? It's not... well, it's not really a barn anymore."

He looked over at the nisse, who was sitting by the fire, darning the old farmer's socks. "No..." he said, sighing. "I guess it ain't."

That evening, they had their Christmas porridge and

exchanged presents. The nisse gave the old farmer a horseshoe he'd found.

"Belonged to Asher... I've had it for a while. He was a good horse," the nisse said. The old man teared up, the way old people do.

"He was the best horse..." he said, "thank you." He blew his nose and handed the nisse a small parcel wrapped in brown paper.

"It's not much," he said, "but there's another present coming on New Year's Eve."

The nisse stared. In his hand, he held a small whittled horse. The finest woodwork he had ever seen, and the horse itself was unmistakable. The posture, the ears, the beautiful saddle. The old farmer had carved him a miniature Asher. The best horse that had ever been on the farm, and the nisse's last proper friend. The two men exchanged a handshake in lieu of having learned how to hug.

"Merry Christmas, old man," said the nisse.

"Merry Christmas, old friend," said the man.

On New Year's Eve, they listened to the radio and ate the rest of the Christmas ham. The farmer's son would be back in two days, and both the farmer and the nisse felt a certain sadness seep through the night.

"I've got something for you," said the farmer. "It's... a very final present, of sorts."

"Right," said the nisse, braced for impact. "I guess it's time for final things..."

It was two minutes to midnight, and the fireworks from the town were already lighting up the sky. They stepped out into the night, and the old man gave the nisse his hand again.

"It's been a pleasure," he said.

"Likewise," said the nisse, before the old man lit a fuse.

He hadn't bought many fireworks. Just a few Roman

Candles, a fountain, and one misplaced ground battery, aimed at an unfortunate angle. The barn was old and the wood brittle, and it burned like kindling in the crisp night air. The fire brigade managed to save the house, but the barn burned right to the ground.

"Good luck out there," he whispered.

"You too," the night whispered back.

Why I deserve presents this Christmas
(no matter what my dad says)

Dear Santa,

I don't believe in you anymore, but I wanted to clear up a couple of misunderstandings, just in case. My dad said that after how I've behaved this year, there's no way in the H-word Santa'd bring me any presents. This is fine as you don't exist, but I don't think it's entirely fair.

I shouldn't have put that mouse in the plastic box with the lid on. I knew it from the second mum shrieked in the kitchen, and had I realised before, I would have come to resuscitate it, as I've learned how at school. But mum had already flung it outside and it landed under my dad's car as he was coming home, and you can't use resuscitation for being squished. I didn't mean to hurt the mouse. It was scuttling around in the kitchen, looking for food, and I remember how grandma said she used to love watching the mice run around when she was little. We were going to visit her the next day, and I thought it would be a nice present for her, to bring the mouse along so she could watch it run.

I know people who are mean to animals often become serial killers, but I want you to know I put plenty of cheese and some napkins in the box before I closed it. I don't know exactly how mice keep their nests, but the hamster we have in the classroom likes burrowing down into soft things, and the napkins were 3-ply – my mum says they're the softest.

That thing with the Schultz's dog was a misunderstanding. I hadn't seen it before and I thought it was lost, and as I know how angry Mrs. Schultz gets when Brandy poops on her lawn, I thought it would be best if I let the dog out so it could find its way home. Had I known it already was home, I wouldn't have opened the gate.

Your elves might have told you I punched Harry Michaels, but that's actually not what happened at all. Have you ever played football? If you have, you know it's not allowed to pull another player's shirt, and it's not really my fault if Harry decided to pull my shirt just as I was turning around. I know Harry says I punched him 'cause he said football's not a sport for girls, but I had already scored two goals, so you tell me if I hadn't already showed him.

'Twasn't me who hid dad's car keys when he needed to catch that plane to Berlin. Honestly, I think he was just stressed 'cause he was running late, and needed someone to blame for the keys being in such a weird place. I would never have hidden them in the fridge, as my mum would have found them sooner or later. I usually hide them in a flowerpot, or somewhere else no one would think to look. That day, I hadn't touched them. My dad was just being unreasonable. I hope this doesn't put him on the naughty list – there's a lot going on in his office, mum says, and he really is trying his best.

Finally – and I hope this doesn't count as tattling – I know everyone thinks Siobhan is *so* wonderful and your elves might never have seen her do anything bad (or are elves allowed to go into girls' changing rooms? How does that work?), but she always makes Clara really sad after gym. And last week, she laughed at Edgar Thompson's drawing until he got all teary and said he needed the bathroom. I guess that doesn't count as naughty as such, but I know both her and Clara want a smartphone for Christmas. Clara's parents will never be able to afford a new one, but Siobhan says she's getting the Samsung 8. Perhaps maybe this once, you could wrap them up wrong, or give both of them a second-hand one – I'm sure Clara won't mind.

I'm sorry I don't believe in you anymore. I'll do my best not to spoil you for my brother. I hope you like the cookies.

Love,

Henrietta Archer, nine and one quarter years old

The creeper in the snow

It always starts the same way. Little by little, you become aware of having a body. It's slow at first, just a feeling of roundness. There's no way of knowing if you're a head or a stomach, or maybe – if they're building you extra tall – what you are at this moment is a chest. Then comes the feeling of being whole. A distinct sensation of knowing what's you and what is not you. Sometimes, there's the gentle heat of stubby little fingers, running all over you, wrapping you in a memory of who you were last time. This heat will harden your outer layer, which means this time will last longer, if you're lucky.

A lot is down to luck, in the end. Good kids give you big, round eyes, brilliant for scoping out the territory. Dim-witted, impatient ones will give you eyes of ice and snow, which splits your vision into thousands of fractals and paints the world in a disorienting blur. Sometimes – the worst times – the kids get called in for dinner before they've given you any eyes at all. Then all you can do is stand there and hope that this is the first snow of winter, so you'll get to melt and start over soon. On those occasions, you never get to find out who you are or what you're meant to be doing.

But if everything goes to plan, and you make it to your first night alive, then you're presented with an identity, your mission brief, and any available intel on the area. That's when the real fun begins.

This year, the first snow came late to Hillcrest Drive, and I was raring to go from the very first touch. Snowman magic is powerful stuff, and I think the kids could sense my eagerness. The youngest kept his distance from me, and insisted his sister gave me smaller eyes. According to him, the big lumps of coal she'd chosen made me too creepy to stand outside his bedroom window. I didn't mind. The two stones she gave me were just the right distance apart. They gave me a perfect, focused view of the world around me, rather than the messy, double-visioned chaos I so often get.

The youngest one stared at me intently. He looked delicious. It was all I could do not to break the code and gulp him down there and then. You always have to wait until nightfall to move. The adults would freak if they knew.

I don't know what it's like for humans, but waiting, as a snowman, is a slow and aching pain. *Not too long now*, I thought. *Not too long now*.

It's rare for children to build us facing their houses. I've often thought that although we've done our very best through the years to keep the truth of our kind hidden, splinters of our consciousness must have leaked out into the world and pierced through into their nightmares. They build us, love us, but they're weary and cautious around us. Find it best to make us looking away.

Something about these two, however, was making the unfamiliar feeling 'the creeps' spread through my densely packed snow.

"You're right," said the eldest one. "It doesn't look kind, even though I gave it a smile.

"So *creepy*," said the youngest one, and shuddered in his massive coat.

"Maybe it's still something about the eyes," said the sister. Without sentiment or caution, she pried the stones out of my face and replaced them with two smooth pebbles.

Ye-e-es, I thought. *Much better*.

"No," the eldest said. "That's not it." And for a few more moments, I was deprived of sight. When it came back, it was without any chance of peripheral vision, as I was now observing the world through the ends of two empty toilet rolls.

"No!" the youngest one whined, "'s'not better. Try with these." He handed his sister two plastic daisies he had nicked from a decoration somewhere. I could hardly see anything, and the world looked back through a yellow haze. I was fuming.

"Oh," said the youngest one. "I think we've made him angry."

"It's all right," said the sister, holding an arm protectively around the boy. "We've got your plan. It'll be okay."

The rest of the evening, I could tell they were staring at me through the window. Every 10 minutes or so, one of their faces appeared behind the glass, making notes on a small piece of paper. But night-time means bedtime, and just as the lights went off in the house, I suddenly understood who I was and what I was meant to do.

I am snowman A-3-44, I thought to myself. *I am being punished for previous misconduct. This is an intel mission only. I will not engage.*

But as soon as I knew it, I knew I'd ignore it. My nature, I now knew, was to disobey orders and eat what I could. Eat children, like in the bad old days. This new vegetarian approach was not one I'd ever support.

We are ancient. We are many. But despite our rules and strict code of conduct, the hive has still not figured out punishment in any lasting way. This is my 42nd mission of punishment; 20-odd years of not engaging, not eating a child – and yet, I haven't gone hungry for a single season. There is nothing they can do.

Someday, I'm sure, they will notify the Queen. They will invent a tribunal or send me to the melter. But our consciousness is eternal. As long as there is snow, there's tomorrow. As long as there's tomorrow, I will feed.

Gathering the necessary information and uploading it to the hive took me seconds. Whenever we're built in a new place, we read weather data and climate reports from the plants and trees around us. Track the weather of the planet, measure its winds and its snow. The past few years' findings have worried the others, but to me, it was all the same. All I cared about was hunger. All that excited me was the chase.

The boy and his sister gave me arms. Long, reaching branches with twigs for fingers and claws. When the darkness was complete, I got to work. Carving out a mouth was easy. Growing teeth was only a question of moving heat around. Icicles stretched like stalactites and stalagmites in my jaws. *It is time*, I thought. *It is time*.

"You were right!" said a voice behind me. "It *is* alive. Like, *properly* alive."

"We should get Daddy," said the other, whimpering and weak.

"Don't be silly," said the elder. "It's just a snowman. Are you sure it's the same one?"

I started turning around. Moving as a snowman is difficult. Our bodies are designed for decoration, not action. But as soon as I faced them, I saw that they had come prepared. The eldest was holding a shovel, the youngest a thick wooden baseball bat. I grinned, exposing my long icy teeth, and rejoiced in the terrified gasps.

"Look!" said the little one, pointing at my feet. "Right there, it's the same mark."

I flipped my head towards him. Confused. Our marks were how we told each other apart. No mortal had ever discovered them before, as far as I knew.

"Oh yeah," said his sister curiously, bending down to take a closer look. She flipped out her notebook, ruffled through the pages, and I could see they had gathered hundreds of our symbols. They'd been scribbled and drawn by just as many children's hands. When she got to the right page, where my symbol was carefully noted next to a warning sign, she nodded to herself and pulled something out of her pocket.

"Badger and Rabbit, this is Pony and Salamander, over."

"Pony and Salamander, this is Badger and Rabbit, we hear you loud and clear, over."

"We've found it," said the girl, keeping half an eye on me. "We found the evil one. Is everything ready? Over."

"Everything's ready," a voice crackled in response. "We'll get Polar Bear and Pussycat, and meet you in 20. Over and out."

It occurred to me, as slow as an avalanche but with the same inevitable certainty, that these kids thought they could fight me. That somehow, they had gotten it into their brains that a shovel and a lump of wood could stop an ancient being from swallowing them whole. I laughed then. The sound dry and horrible, the creaking of footsteps in snow.

The girl sighed. "We're on to you, you know. We've been tracking you lot for years. We know that you're the evil one and that you eat children instead of gingerbread men like the others." She looked at me, scraping her shovel absentmindedly at the snow, tilting her head as if she was waiting for me to respond.

"Don't make it angry!" said the little one. "Let's just wait for the others, okay?"

His sister shrugged. "Whatever," she said. "It just annoys me that he's grinning like that."

I could smell the boy from where I stood, his fear spreading through the air like fine perfume. My stomach growled, and although I was curious to see what the children thought they were doing, I decided I couldn't wait any longer. I pried my jaws up and apart, and started gurgling the sacred chant.

"Oh, shut up," said the sister, using the handle of her shovel to punch in my teeth.

"It was gonna try to eat me!" said the little one, half hiding behind his elder sister. "I don't think it knows!"

"I think you're right," said the sister. "That's really weird. I wonder if they're all like that. Thinking everything's like normal..."

My mouth hurt. My jaw was struggling to grow new teeth, my snow reeling from the shock. I tried to keep my emotion under control, as rage can melt us from the inside, but I knew now that I wouldn't just *eat* the boy. I would tear him apart limb from limb, after doing the same to his sister.

I stretched my arm out, ready to throttle her, and found her to be further away than I thought. Inching forward, the ground dropped beneath me.

"Easy there," the girl said, catching me gently in her arms, which were suddenly all too big for her small size.

Only then, as I caught our reflection in the window pane, did I realise what they had done. I was tiny. Not much bigger than a doll. They had propped me up on a bird feeder so they could keep an eye on me from the house, but even with my full strength and snowman magic, these silly little twigs wouldn't even be able to wrap around her wrist.

I roared. Wriggling and wrestling and trying to bite my way free of her grasp. My only hope now was falling. Falling hard enough to break apart into pieces too small to hold my self. Start again somewhere else.

She put me down on the ground, and kept me in place by using the shovel to drag me this way and that.

"You might as well just take it easy," she said. "We're not going to let you go. It's taken us *ages* to get you here. Look," she said, scooping me up on the shovel and turning me out towards the garden.

And there they were. Dozens and dozens of my brethren, covering the lawn in miniature forms, looking shyly away from my peril. I called to them then, unable to hide a twinge of pleading from my voice. But they remained silent, a choir of judgment, feeling I would finally get my punishment.

The other kids showed up, inspecting my mark and laughing at my futile attempts at escape. The girl was clearly their ringleader, passing out tasks and having me propped up in a padded box, put on a sleigh they pulled towards town.

"Have you got the key?" she asked one of the newcomers, a chubby kid who didn't seem to fear me at all.

He held up a keychain, proudly rattling it in the night. "Got it," he said, as if it wasn't self-evident.

It hadn't occurred to me to worry, not really. I couldn't imagine a single place these children could take me that would pose any real danger to me. But something didn't feel right. Everywhere we passed, each garden's snowman seemed to watch our parade, as if they knew we were coming. As if they knew where we were going.

"And you're absolutely sure no one will take him out?" said the ringleader, watching nervously as the chubby kid unlocked the door in front of us.

"One hundred *thousand* percent. Unless Dad sells the store, this box will be safe in the freezer. I can't remember the last time they even cleaned it, to be honest."

"Eww..." said the others, but the boy just shrugged.

"Comes in handy, dunnit?" he said, prying the door open.

"We have to move quickly so it doesn't start melting, okay?" said the girl, lifting the box out and running me through a large convenience store. When they got to the freezer room. They placed me behind crates upon crates of microwave meals, frozen vegetables and seafood.

The girl crouched down in front of me. "The snow queen told us it might take a couple of seasons," she said, "but if you're in here long enough, you'll probably forget. Do you see?" she said, pointing to the images they'd drawn all around the box. "These are snowmen. Nice little things with top hats and magic that keep children company at Christmas. You'll forget about your past and start to think you're one of them."

The youngest one came closer, still holding himself a step or two away from me but nearer now than he had been before. "Here," he said shyly. "I brought you this in case you get hungry." He dropped two gingerbread men into the box, then hesitated a second before pulling a paper doll out of his pocket. "And this," he said, placing it gently into the box. "In case it gets lonely in here."

And then the hours started passing. Followed by the days and weeks and months. This place feels more like home now. It smells faintly of gingerbread, and I have friends on every wall. I know I'm praying for a powercut, some way to get outside. I can't quite remember why, or where I feel I need to go, but there's something I need to do out there. Someone I need to visit. The thought of it makes me hungry, and my teeth grow long and hard.

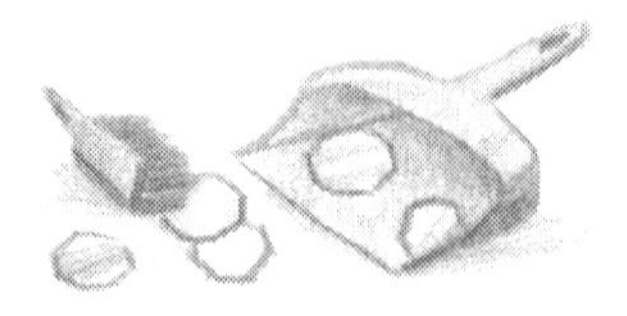

The curious case of the glitter men

Creation is a curious thing. Thousands of ideas float around in the ether, looking for willing hosts. They grow and mature until it's time, then they seek their way into the world. It's a good system – full of light and creativity – but it isn't flawless.

Often, ideas grow so big they find their way into multiple hosts at the same time. An inventor in Austria and another in Texas will arrive at the same invention within days of each other, causing legal battles and accusations of theft. The mobile phone was nowhere at all, then everywhere else all at once. Science, art and invention – they all know this to be true. Ideas are out there, and when they're ready, they come. If you catch one, you'd better bring it to life real quick, or someone else will do it first.

Sometimes, however, ideas crash into sparks of creation and become living entities of their own. Such was the case of the glitter men. Mind you, it started as something else completely. In fact, it was the idea of sanitary services that was about to come true. Litter men, bin men, people whose job it would be to pick up other people's litter and bring it out of town. The idea had set off for Earth, ready to come to life, but halfway there, it had gotten stuck. Its limbs got tangled with that of another idea. It was the idea of slang it crashed into, although what slang was doing this close to Earth is a bit of a mystery. It wasn't yet ready to make its way down.

By pure coincidence, a spark of creation was zooming about that day. It was bored and restless, desperate to create. It was a young spark. It zipped past the two struggling ideas, wondering what they were doing. It zipped past two or three times before curiosity got the better of it. What will happen, it thought, if I crash into them both at once?

On its next round, it sped up. It hurled itself into the unsuspecting concepts with all its might, rejoicing as sparks and thunder roared, and the ideas were torn apart.

Poor things. The idea of slang had its G ripped off, and fell to the ground as slan'. Suddenly people were droppin' and poppin' and groovin' all over. Slang hadn't meant for it to go this way, but now that it had, there was nothing it could do about it.

The idea of litter men fell to earth with the G stuck to its face. Unable to see where it was going, it flailed and screamed as it thrashed through the freezing air and into a pocket in time and space. There, it went through the roof of Father Christmas, who smiled with his eyes above the rim of his glasses.

"What are you, then?" he said, having met ideas before, "let's take a look." He helped the idea to its feet, brushed it off and laughed.

"Glitter men? What a strange idea... All right, let's see where we can put them." The idea began to take form, and followed Father Christmas into one of his many workshops.

"What about here?" he said, pointing down to a corner full of doll-sized bunk beds. "This can be your base, I suppose. I've got a load of witch dolls somewhere, we could take the brooms from them, and bins... well... maybe you could use baskets instead, and we can take them from the hot air balloons?" he suggested, watching as the idea split apart into a small army of old men.

All of them were wearing dull, grey jumpsuits with unexplained grease stains on the arms. They each grabbed a witch's broom and a basket, then filed into motorised toy garbage trucks – four in each – and set off into the world.

"Right..." said Father Christmas, chuckling in his beard. "Wonder how long this one'll last. Will be like those digital pets, I'm sure."

The glitter men came out at night all over the world. They traced the steps of young women in party dresses, picking up flecks of glitter from the floor. They lingered around the heads of five year olds, as no matter what they had done during the day, at night, they all seemed to be covered in glitter. Some of the glitter men visited the sites of birthday parties, scraping glitter off the table where cards had been lined up. The luckiest ones got to step in under Christmas trees. There, they could sometimes fill a truck at a time.

"Now what, Boss?" the foreman said when they returned to the North Pole. Father Christmas looked out over the many trucks, and the buckets full of glitter they'd collected.

"Well..." he said, scratching his beard, "I suppose we could use it for the Christmas cards... Take them to the vats."

"Yes, Boss," said the foreman, and yelled out a set of orders so thick and garbled that only other glitter men knew what he meant. They set up shop in the vats, sorted the glitter by colour and texture.

"This is great," said the elf who was managing director of the card factory, "and very environmentally friendly to recycle like this."

"Ayup," said the foreman.

Glitter gets everywhere. It cascades from even the best secured surface but will stick to your skin for eternity. The bin men knew this the way all craftsmen know things about their craft they never remember learning, just feel they've always known.

Glitter collection became an art form. The best glitter men could identify single specks of glitter in a hotel carpet within milliseconds, pick it up and be onto the next gig before the next millisecond came about. They used Father Christmas's magic to move around, being everywhere at once before they even got there. The card factory vats were a sight for sore eyes. And if your eyes weren't sore, they might become sore from looking at the thousands of reflections in all the colours of the rainbow.

It wasn't the idea's fault, of course. It hadn't meant to become what it was. But soon, the glitter men began disappearing. They were all old men, and time ran its course. As no new glitter men were born or created, within a few years, there was only the foreman left.

"Now what, Boss?" he said to Father Christmas, who stared at him with intense curiosity.

"Now, who are you then?" he said. He didn't mean to be rude, it's just the way stories go. The very idea of glitter men was fading from his memory like all unfulfilled ideas eventually do. "You new here?" he said.

The foreman looked at him with sad eyes. "Ayup," he said, then disappeared with a pop. Father Christmas blinked. He felt like he had been in a conversation, but couldn't remember who with.

"We've got a problem," the managing director of the card factory said. "We're running out of glitter. The vats are almost empty and we don't know where to get more."

Father Christmas sighed.

"The world is full of glitter that people have dropped," he said, "wouldn't it be great if we had a way to collect it all? Bring it back here and use it again?"

"You mean like a recycling service?" the elf said, wrinkling his forehead in an attempt to keep up.

"I guess," said Father Christmas. "You know... like a renovation service. Bin men and women, but for glitter."

"Don't you mean g-litter men," the elf joked.

"Ho ho ho," said Father Christmas, who quite appreciated a good pun. "But yes, Alfred, glitter men. Isn't that a good idea?" Then he blinked. Remembering something.

"Don't we have glitter men on our payroll already?" he said, and they both turned to the foreman, who stood there, watching the conversation with interest.

"Ayup," said the foreman, and got back to work.

The banner of the walnut, buckle and comb

The Inn by the Three Roads was usually quite busy. Travellers going from Borinne to Yravall, or passing through Yravall on their way to Aufsted, would often rest there on their way.

The inn was the surest way to get fresh news this side of the mountains, and the innkeeper was a goodhearted man who let poorer travellers set their tents and wagons up behind the building. When the gentry and merchants had finished what they'd paid for, he would bring the pot outside and let the wanderers, tinkers and travelling folks

share the rest for a few coppers.

In reality, he did this out of more than just the goodness of his heart. The innkeeper loved music. He loved it with a passion so pure it didn't matter much if the music was performed by a fiddler from the village or a court troubadour – Master Steele would adore it either way. By being generous to his poorer lodgers, the inn often had music at night from travelling troupes, although he retained the more fashionable clientele by keeping the lodgings high-end.

Now, however, it was the second day of the winter festival, and the roads were all but deserted. A few traders had stopped by earlier in the morning, but had hurried onward to make it home in time for the evening's presents and goose. Just as well, they came to experience, as a storm was rolling down the mountainside. Soon, the inn was the only visible proof that there was a road going through this pass. The ground was covered in a thick, even layer of snow, and the furious flurries hid all trace of life.

The innkeeper sighed. He should have followed his own gut and not put so much food on the boil. He had held out hope that there would be a guest or two to share his meal, but it looked like he'd be dining alone. *Blessed festival*, he thought, and poured himself a generous helping of honey mead.

The storm was picking up. The shutters rattled on their hinges, the roof creaked and groaned from the unfamiliar weight of snow. Every now and then, a strong gust would force its way down the chimney and blow smoke into the room, and the wind whistled through some of the cracks around windows and doors. But other than that, he was quite lucky, he thought. He was safe and warm. There was plenty of food, and... yes, there seemed to be company coming.

Even with his broad shoulders and steady gait, he

struggled to keep himself upright against the wind. He pushed his way across the yard and out to where a young man was struggling to get a horse through the snow.

"Come this way, lad," he shouted above the howling wind. "You've stepped off the road, this is no weather for travelling." The young man looked up at him, his face pale and lips blue from frost. There was significant bruising along one cheek, the innkeeper noticed, and the young man's fine clothing was dishevelled, as if he'd needed to stay on horseback for a very long time.

"I... I... I...'ve... got no... money," he stuttered through clattering teeth.

"No matter," the innkeeper said, helping him guide the terrified horse to the stables. "I can't very well let you die out here."

They got the horse inside, dried it off and covered it with a light blanket. The innkeeper offered it two measures of oats, and an apple, as it was a special night.

"Blessed festival," he said, patting the horse's neck. The young man was shivering violently, and the innkeeper made him some bitter tea and gave him a seat by the fire.

"I should really get going," the man stuttered, his hands struggling to hold the mug steady. "My party... we were... I need to... and my ma', she'll..."

"She'd rather have you alive and well," the innkeeper said, pushing the man gently back in his chair. "There's no use going back out there tonight, lad. It'll be the death of both you and your horse. Stay here, share a meal with me, and tomorrow morn' we'll have you on your way as soon as the weather clears."

The innkeeper began to set a table for the two of them. Outside, the blinding white daylight was giving way to the blue hues of early dusk. Against the darkening evening, the innkeeper noticed a flickering yellow light reflecting off the trees. There were no windows to the back, so if he wanted to find the source he would have to head outside. He sighed. It wasn't a tempting proposition, but if there was a fire raging nearby, it would be worse not to know.

A grey tent was drooping heavily under the snow, and two women sat huddled by a small camp fire. It was shielded in the gap between two boulders, but even so, the innkeeper couldn't imagine much heat would radiate through the gale.

"Ladies," he called, stomping through the snow that now stretched to his knees, "please come inside. We're just about to have our dinner if you care to share." The youngest of them turned to him. Her cheeks were marbled red from the cold, and the ends of her hair hung stiff and frozen from the moisture in her breath.

"Thank you for the offer," she said, her heavy accent revealing she was a Gernlender, "but we will be fine with our fire."

The older lady spoke to her in Gerndish, her voice pleading and hectic. The youngest shook her head, cut off the elder with a few words, clutching the brooch of her travelling cloak.

They're troubadours, the innkeeper thought. He was surprised, but knew better than to show it. He bowed deeply.

"My ladies," he said, holding the bow, "excuse my clumsy wording. I am not offering to help, but rather asking for the pleasure of your company. Bring your instruments inside to keep them from turning, and accept my humble meal. Should the spirit speak to you, I would be delighted to hear you perform later tonight. I will pay guild rates," he added hurriedly.

The young woman's eyes flickered from the innkeeper to the tent a couple of times. He kept his face mild, although he struggled to keep from running back inside. *I'm going to freeze my plums off if she doesn't decide soon*, he thought, but he forced himself to stay relaxed and easy.

Troubadours were usually wealthy enough to pay for his rooms, and he couldn't be blamed for mistaking them for regular travelling musicians, sitting out in the snow as they were. If troubadours were good enough, they'd travel with the credentials of some Jarl or Duke of the kingdoms, and the innkeeper could trust that the beneficiary would settle their bill with time. They must have fallen on bad times, these two, to be out here alone without a troupe, a wagon or credentials. *Probably between banners*, he thought, *or they were troubadours under the blue and fox...*

The elder of the two stood up, ignoring the youngest's objections.

"We will happily grace you with our company, Master..." the old lady said, her accent even thicker than the younger's.

"Steele," the innkeeper said, bowing again. "I am honoured." He helped them carry their few belongings – the tent, rolled up, an instrument case and two travel sacks – and led them inside to the fire, where the young man jumped up to greet them.

"We've got more company, lad," the innkeeper said. "Ladies, this is... you know, I don't think I got your name."

The young man looked at him for a moment, then bowed to the women. "It's an honour," he said, "You can call me Daniel."

The women nodded their heads. "I'm Myrabelle D'Chare," the youngest said, "and this is my mother, Ysabelle D'Chare."

"Whose banner do you travel under?" the boy asked, seeing no colour or stamp of patronage. The women exchanged a glance.

"We've been travelling under the blue and fox," the younger said, keeping her head high, fixing Daniel with a stare. The innkeeper nodded to himself. That did indeed explain their ragged appearance.

The blue and fox was Duke Lehmann's banner. He had been tried for treason last season, after a spy had come forward with information about his questionable loyalties. His land and dependencies had been returned to the Aufstedian king, who in turn had given them to the Duke of Odelberg, who was currently in favour. The Duke of Odelberg had not, however, kept any of Duke Lehmann's credentials active. This had forced scores of artists, troubadours, mercenaries, ladies in waiting and members of the court to seek elsewhere, finding themselves unwanted by anyone who hoped to keep on the Duke of Odelberg's good side – which was most people, in these trying times.

The innkeeper set the table for four as his guests got their heat back by the fire. The young man was an excellent conversationalist, and seemed used to speaking to members of the court. The women were polite and friendly, keeping the conversation going with tales of the four kingdoms and places they'd been. Had it not been for the lack of clinging coin in the innkeepers till, he would have felt he was an intruder in a social gathering where he didn't belong.

"I'm afraid there's no festival goose," he said as he carried the stew over to the table, "but the meat is good, the bread is fresh and the mead is the best in the area. I'm honoured and pleased to share my food with you this night. Blessed festival." He raised his mug to toast them.

"Blessed festival," they smiled and toasted him back, and throughout the meal they thanked him over and over again for his kindness, and complimented his mead and food.

"It is traditional," he said, when everyone had finished their food, and sat happy and full in their chairs, "that the host present small gifts with the pudding at the winter festival." He smiled at his guests.

"Oh, Master Steele, you've given us quite enough," said Ysabelle.

"Yes, dear Master Steele, your generosity is already well and truly above and beyond anything I've come to expect along this road," said Daniel, touching his heart in the way of Borinnian noblemen.

"Ah," said the innkeeper, holding a finger in the air, "but the purpose of the gifts is not to establish the generosity of the host, but the worth of his guests," he said. Then sighed. "But I am a humble man, and I fear my gifts will not be what you three are used to in terms of refinement or value." All three set out to protest, but the innkeeper lifted his hand again, gently persuading them to hear him out. "And therefore," he continued, "I must ask you to see beyond the immediate worth and rather look to how they reflect my regard for you all." He looked down, a little hesitantly, then pulled his three gifts out onto the table.

"Madame Ysabell," he said, starting with the eldest as was tradition, "for you, have I have a walnut and the buckle from my second belt." He handed them to her, his hands shaking a little. She accepted them politely, but exchanged a glance of concern with the others.

"I thank you, Master Steele..." she started, but he interrupted her.

"The case for your harp," he said gesturing to the corner of the room. "It's been badly scratched from your travels. The walnut will help take the worst of the scratches out; just rub the walnut down the grooves, then wait for a few moments before polishing it all. It won't fix it completely, of course, but it will help mask the worst of it." He swallowed. "And I noticed one of your clasps has come loose," he pointed to the side of the harp case where one of the clasps hung freely along the side. "The buckle from my belt will replace it until you are back on your feet." She looked at him, her eyes warm with gratefulness and compassion.

"Thank you Master Steele," she said. "That is a most thoughtful gift."

He turned his attention to the young man.

"Master David," he said, "I noticed your horse had some bad sores under her saddle. I take it you've had a rough ride, and have encountered troubles on your way. For you, I have a saddle blanket I cut from my old travelling cloak. It's in a thick and soft weave, and I've treated it with crest-willow sap so it will help her heal."

David stood up and bowed deeply to the innkeeper. "Thank you, Master Steele," he said. "This gift is generous and most welcome."

"Finally," said the innkeeper, "Madame Myrabelle, I offer you this..." He handed a small, decorative wooden comb to the young lady. It was a simple comb, missing two teeth and darkened from years of use, in the shape of a large rose.

"I realise it doesn't look like much, but it belonged to my wife, gods bless her soul, and she treated it with mennas oil to help keep her hair soft and shiny. It's one of the few things she had that... that she held dear." He smiled a sad little smile, and stretched out for her to take the comb. She hesitated, but eventually picked it up and gave him a stiff smile in return.

As soon as he left to get the pudding, she dropped the comb onto the table.

"That is a lillywood comb," her mother said, "it is also a memory of his dead wife, and a practical gift for a girl whose hair bears clear markings of road dust and hard times. He's honoured you with something quite valuable – even from a monetary point of view, he would be able to sell that comb for half a silver. Lillywood is rare, and it's fine craftsmanship even though it's missing a tooth here and there. Do not disrespect him or the gift. He has shown you a great honour." She fixed her daughter with a stern stare.

"I'm sorry," the daughter said, blushing slightly and pushing the comb deep into her hair.

"It looks good on you," the young man said, deepening the blush further.

The pudding was dense and good, with plenty of fruit throughout. The innkeeper offered them drinks and biscuits, and they all retired to the chairs by the fire, feeling warm and content. The storm had quieted down somewhat, but the snow was still falling heavily outside.

"I believe we promised you we would play," Madame Ysabelle said after a while. "But are you sure you want to risk it, us being former servants of the blue and fox? Whose lands are these... The young Lord Segreve, I believe?"

The innkeeper shook his head. "No, my lady. This is my land. I own this inn and the land it stands on, and here, banners don't matter. Besides, from what I hear, our Lord Segreve is a decent man. I'm sure he wouldn't mind."

"You could get in trouble," the lady cautioned.

"I could. But it would be wrong for me to get in trouble, and right for me to let you play."

The young man gave him a curious look, perhaps surprised at the innkeeper's disobedience. Keeping with the rules of the area's Lord was important. Vital, in some cases. But he didn't protest.

"Then we play," the lady said.

Madame Ysabelle opened her case – now shining smoothly after Master Steele had helped her polish it – and tuned the harp, slowly and patiently. Her daughter took a few deep swigs of water and walked across the room to warm up her voice. When the old lady began playing, it wasn't a simple tune sliding out of her instrument. It wasn't the plinking clamour of a travelling musician's instrument or the hard tune of the church's musicians. What weaved through the room was a soft melody, each tone so round and friendly it filled their minds completely. The daughter's voice held some of the same quality. It was full, vibrant and rich, but mellow like a smooth pebble in summer sun. The song ran counter to the harp's melody. They crossed each other, went against each other, filled out each other's quiet stretches with harmonious interludes. The technical difficulty would have been obvious to anyone who had studied music, but they made it sound effortless and simple.

The innkeeper wept, the music moving him to his very core. Master Daniel listened with his eyes closed, his hands tracing the music in the air and reaching for it when the last few notes flew through between them and lingered in each of their hearts.

"That was beautiful," the innkeeper said, bowing to them and kissing their hands. "Thank you."

It was three days before the roads opened up and the visitors could be on their way. The innkeeper took care of them, fed them and offered them his best rooms. The four of them got along well, and kept each other company through the long evenings. After dinner, the women would play, and never had they played for such an appreciative audience.

On the fourth day, the innkeeper packed them all lunches. He took the eldest troubadour aside and paid her the full rate for four nights of music. She tried to protest, but he insisted, hoping the handful of coins would help them get back onto their feet.

"Blessed festival," he said, waving them goodbye after many rounds of sincere thanks and best wishes. "Must all your roads be short and easy to tread, and your days good ones!"

He missed them when they left. The roads were still thick with snow, and he didn't see many customers over the next few days. But he kept the memory of the music in his heart, and he hummed along to the remembered tunes for days.

Two full cycles turned, and the usual hustle and bustle of the road picked back up. The Inn by the Three Roads was its usual humming self when the door was flung open, blowing a hush over the gathered crowd. Lord Segreve himself stepped into to the open room, followed by guards and advisers.

"Where is the man called Master Steele?" he called.

"Here," said the innkeeper, not looking up. He had been dreading this moment for years. The day his disregard for banners would lead to trouble.

"What can I get for you, my Lord? The honey mead is particularly fine," he said, turning to polish another glass. The crowd held its breath. They too had been expecting this moment.

"Master Steele, I have come to repay my debt to you," the Lord said, now standing right in front of the innkeeper behind the bar.

"I don't believe you owe me anything, my Lord," the innkeeper said, unsure where this was going. There was a defiance in his stance the regulars hadn't seen before. He looked braced for impact.

When he finally met the young Lord's eye, there was only a brief flicker of recognition before he nodded.

"I trust your mare got home all right?" he said.

"Yes, the saddle blanket helped, and her back healed up

nicely," the Lord said, smiling broadly.

"I'm afraid I cannot stay," said the Lord. "But I have brought a gift to repay you for your kindness and hospitality."

One of his clerks held out a scroll of parchment.

"I thought for sure you were here to bring me up on charges of letting the blue and fox's troubadours play on your land. You seemed so torn by the consideration," said Master Steele, reaching for the parchment.

"This isn't my land," the Lord smiled, "this is your land."

"Yes, well… you know what I mean," said Master Steele, trying to wring his head around the impressive lettering on the scroll.

"Yes, I do," said the Lord. "And perhaps… had the circumstances been different, I would have been insulted. But you took me in that night, without knowing who I was, without the offer of pay or reward. You treated me kindly, you didn't ask who I was or where I came from. I have no doubt I would have frozen to death had you not allowed me inside."

The innkeeper nodded. "Aye, you were getting quite blue."

"So I have issued you this letter of credentials," the Lord continued, "and a seal to hang above your door. It details that troubadours travelling grey – those whose banners have been disbanded, and those who are in between banners alike – can play freely at the Inn of the Three Roads, under the protection of Lord Segreve and the man they call Master Steele."

"Here," he said, giving the man another present. It was a folded up piece of fabric. The Lord had two of his guards unfold it and hold it up against the wall. It was a beautiful banner – grey like the banner of the bannerless, but depicting a walnut, a buckle and a comb.

"The musicians playing here can play under their own banner, if it is welcome in the area. Or..." he said, smiling, "they can play under the banner of the walnut, buckle and comb. The wages of which will be paid by me, in a yearly stipend to your inn." He grinned.

"But tonight," he said, pointing to the door where Ysabelle and Myrabelle was stepping in. "I would be grateful if you could put up the newest troubadours playing under my banner. They have a great fondness for this inn."

The women came up and bowed to Master Steele. Myrabelle had his wife's comb tucked in her beautiful raven black hair.

Master Steele stood with his mouth open, confused and baffled by this enormous honour. He bowed back to the two ladies, and his heart filled with joy at the thought of another night of their music.

The Inn of the Three Roads was always busy. Travellers going from Borinne to Yravall, or passing through Yravall on their way to Aufsted would go out of their way to stop there. The inn had the best music and the best honey mead in the four kingdoms. The innkeeper was a good-hearted man, allowing troubadours from every banner to play under his own. Rich and poor alike would gather in what was affectionately called the inn of thieves. So called because it would steal your heart.

A present for Grandma

"It's like a secret mission," Dad had said when he dropped Clara off at Granny and Grandpa's house. "Just listen out for anything she says that sounds like she wants something. Maybe ask to see her jewellery and see if she says, 'I wish I had some blue earrings, but these green ones are all I have,' – or something. You know... just find out what she'd like for Christmas, without asking her."

Clara had said she would, although she had no idea why it had to be such a mystery. Surely, it would have been easier to just ask, like normal people did.

"No," Dad had explained, "Granny always says she wants everyone to be happy. Or she says she needs new socks, or to have her tires changed. Even Grandpa can't get anything sensible out of her. But it would be nice to get her something she wants for once, not just something she needs." He'd been like this since the divorce. Finding little projects he simply wouldn't let go of. So Clara had sighed and agreed, and now she was sitting here, rummaging through Granny's jewellery and asking questions about each piece.

"Just don't suggest getting rid of the horrid Christmas tree brooch," was the last thing Dad had said before driving away. "She loves that thing, and there's nothing we can do about it."

So far, the conversation had been relatively fruitless.

"When did you get these, Granny?"

"Oh, your Gramps gave me those for our second anniversary. Aren't they lovely?"

"Do you wish they were blue?"

"No, I prefer green earrings. All of my earrings are green. I don't know why, I just like the way they make me look," Gran said, and then giggled a little.

"They bring out your eyes," said Grandpa behind his newspaper, and Granny grinned.

"Maybe that's why," she said.

"What about this necklace?" Clara said. "It's broken. Do you want a new one?"

"Oh, no," Granny said. "It's not broken, it's just missing a stone. I like that. It reminds me of when I lost it. It was such a good evening, do you remember?" she said, swatting at Grandpa's leg with her crossword magazine. "Your gramps almost got into a fight over me."

"Oh, now," said Grandpa. "I didn't like the way he talked to you, is all."

Granny giggled, and it was a nice sound, thought Clara. It made her sound much younger, all of a sudden.

The Christmas brooch was the next piece of jewellery, and Clara lifted it gently. It really wasn't very pretty, the shiny paint was half worn off, and it seemed to have been quite garish to begin with. Some of the little glass beads had fallen off, and the stripes that were supposed to be tinsel were worn down to matte, grey metal. But Clara liked the brooch anyway. Granny had worn it on Christmas Eve all of Clara's life. And every year, Dad would sigh and ask her to take it off, and every year, Granny would smile and say that it made her happy to wear it on Christmas Eve.

"Granny?" Clara said. They'd been quiet for a long time, and Granny had returned to her crosswords. "Why do you always wear this tree, even though it's so... eh..." Clara tried to find the right word.

"Tatty, ratty, makes you look batty," Grandpa rhymed, peeking over his paper at Grandma.

"Oh, now!" Granny said, and smacked Grandpa's knee with her magazine. "Someone won't be getting a biscuit with their tea later."

Grandpa lowered his paper and winked to Clara. "Don't worry," he said in a really loud whisper, "I know where she hides the best ones, anyway." Clara laughed.

"The brooch makes me happy, I'll have you both know," Granny said, and stood up to go and make the tea.

"I know," said Clara, "it makes me happy too. But I was wondering why it makes you happy. Did Grandpa give it to you?"

Grandpa laughed. "No, my girl, that's the only piece of jewellery she's kept from one of her boyfriends before me. Must have been some boyfriend too, to keep her wearing it all these years. I think she's still waiting for him to come back," he said, but winked again to show he was joking.

"It wasn't like that," Grandma said, stroking her hands down her apron a few times.

"Granny!" Clara laughed. "You're blushing! Was it really an old boyfriend? Did you love him more than Grandpa? Do you wish he was your husband? What was his name?"

Grandpa folded up his paper and crossed his arms.

"Yes, tell us everything," he said.

Grandma scoffed and stepped into the kitchen, scrambled loudly with mugs and the kettle.

"She can't stay in there forever," Grandpa whispered. Clara wasn't sure if she should feel bad. She didn't want to force gran to say anything she didn't want to, but Grandpa seemed to think it was fine, so it couldn't be that bad, could it?

"It was nothing like that," Grandma shouted from the kitchen, "He was just a good friend." Grandpa and Clara exchanged glances, and Grandpa grinned.

"Here we go," he said, and leaned forward as if something exciting was about to happen.

"His name was Yeromy, and he lived in the flat above us, back in Liverpool," Gran said, coming back out with mugs and biscuits on a tray. "His father worked at the factory with my mum, and his mother did people's laundry, I believe." She poured the tea and dropped two sugars in Clara's mug, even though they both knew she was only allowed one.

"Help yourself to a biscuit," she said, "they're the good kind." She kissed Grandpa on the cheek and sat back down in her pink chair. She closed her eyes, resting her nose on the edge of her mug, the way she always did.

"Yeromy and I used to play together after school, every day, and we were very close. There's nothing wrong with that, I'll have you know."

"Sounds nice!" said Clara.

"He was very nice. He had such fine, black curls too. I used to think he was quite handsome, as a matter of fact, even though it wasn't anything like that."

Grandpa pretended to look offended, and Clara giggled.

"Not as handsome as you, idiot," Grandma sighed. "You're dumber than bread, but you're quite dashing."

"Hah!" said Grandpa. "I haven't dashed anywhere in decades. I'm barely meandering." Clara didn't get it, and grandma rolled her eyes.

"When we were eight, Yeromy and his family had to move to Newcastle. The factory had closed down, and my mum went to work for the lawyer, but Yeromy's father couldn't find any work nearby. It was right before Christmas, and everyone was very upset. The whole neighbourhood worked at the factory, it seemed, and suddenly we were all even poorer than before. We were all right, of course, but..."

Grandma sighed. "Either way. Yeromy's father could get work in Newcastle, but had to start on Christmas Day. They were going to leave on December 23rd, and the night before, Yeromy and I snuck out to the back yard. We'd made ourselves a little shelter there, behind some rubbish in the corner. It was snowing, or perhaps I just think it was, but we crawled into the small space, sat down next to each other, and I swear there were snowflakes melting in his eyelashes.

"'I have a present for you,' he said, and held out a little black, velvet box. 'Open it now.'

"'Oh!' I said. 'I didn't get you anything.' But Yeromy just smiled, and put the box in my hands. He was very proud of the present, I think. He sometimes got a few coins for helping the caretaker – Mr. Johnson, I think it was – rake the leaves or pick up cigarette butts and that sort of thing. Everyone loved Yeromy. He was very helpful, you know. But he must have saved for a long time to afford to buy me anything like that.

"I thought it was the most beautiful thing I'd ever seen. It glittered more back then, and it had all its stones.

"'Wait here!' I said. My eyes were filling with tears and I didn't want him to see me cry. I said, 'Don't go okay?

Promise you won't.' I begged him and he nodded, looking so serious.

"'Mum!' I shouted when I got in, forgetting that I wasn't supposed to be out of bed.

"'What's wrong?' said Mum. She was in her nightgown and so beautiful.

"'I need the Christmas dove, please,' I said, sobbing and howling like a child... which I suppose I was.

"'What do you mean? Why were you outside? What's going on, young lady – tell me right now,' she said.

"'Yeromy,' I sobbed. 'He's leaving tomorrow, and I have no present for him, and he gave me a treasure, and now I can't thank him if I don't get the Christmas dove!'"

Grandma smiled a little and looked at Clara.

"Your great grandmother was a very clever woman, Clara," she said. "You remind me a lot of her."

"I do?"

"Yes. She was always asking good questions, and she didn't have much time for silliness. But she looked at me that evening, and I think she understood that for me, Yeromy moving away was the most important thing that had ever happened to me.

"'Okay, my dove,' she said, and went into the living room. The Christmas dove hung on the Christmas tree. It was a frail porcelain dove with a red ribbon. Your great-grandmother had given it to me a few years before, and I loved it dearly. I felt so proud when I got to put it on the tree. My mum wrapped it in two layers of silk paper and handed it to me.

"'I expect you back inside in ten minutes,' she said sternly.

"'But...'

"'Ten minutes!' And I knew she meant it."

Grandma went quiet for a while, sipped her tea and

chewed her biscuit. Clara hardly dared to breathe, she didn't want the story to end.

"He was still waiting for me," Grandma said. "He was nervous, I think. Perhaps he thought I didn't like his gift, or that something had happened when I went inside. But he had stayed.

"'Here's something for you,' I said, and held the Christmas dove out. I felt embarrassed by the wrapping paper, grey tissue paper my mum used for everything. But he unwrapped it as if the paper was gold leaf, slowly and gently, making sure he wouldn't tear anything.

"'It's beautiful,' he said.

"'It's a Christmas dove,' I said. 'You should hang it up at Christmas.'

"'And you should wear that tree at Christmas.'

"'We'll be Christmas friends,' I said.

"'Best Christmas friends,' he said. And then he kissed me on the cheek and ran away." Grandma stopped.

"And that's that," she said, smiled weirdly and grabbed another biscuit. Clara swallowed.

"What do you mean, that's that? What happened next?"

"He moved to Newcastle," said Grandma and she shrugged. "Never saw him again. Our mums wrote Christmas cards for a few years, but nothing more than that."

"But you kept wearing the tree..." Clara whispered.

"Of course!" Grandpa said, and winked. "They're best Christmas friends."

"Do you not want to see him again, Gran?" said Clara.

"Oh, I don't know what happened to him," said Gran. "He may be dead for all I know. Loads of people who are as old as I am are dead now..."

"You're not that old," said Clara. "I wonder if he kept the dove..."

"Oh, I'm sure he didn't," Grandma scoffed. "He was

just a boy. Anyway. That's why I wear the tree. Now, who wants to play some cards?"

"Did you have a nice time?" Dad asked when he picked Clara up that evening.

"I know what you need to get Grandma," she said, buckling in. "It's a man called Yeromy."

"What?"

"The Christmas brooch was a gift from a boy she grew up with. His name was Yeromy. He moved right before Christmas and gave her the brooch, and she hasn't spoken to him since. But she'd like to."

Dad scratched his beard. "Well... do you know his surname?"

"No."

"Do you know where he is now?"

"Nope."

"Do you know what he looks like or if he has any family?"

"Nope and nope."

"Then I don't know if there's that much I can do," Dad said, "Maybe we should just..."

"Dad?" Clara said. "I think you can do anything."

The next two weeks felt like a movie. Dad went all in. He called the descendants of the factory owners to see if they had kept the employment records from the '50s. They hadn't. Then he called Uncle Edwin to see if he remembered Yeromy's surname, but he didn't remember Yeromy at all. He called the schools in the area, who weren't allowed to give him a name, but could confirm that there had been a Yeromy in his mother's class.

The following Saturday, Clara and Dad took the train to Newcastle to go on the local radio show. Clara told the story as best she could, and one of the hosts – who spoke so fast that Clara could barely understand him – said the most effort he had ever made to give his gran a present was to go to M&S during the sales. The other host – who had a different voice when she spoke into the microphone than when she spoke to Clara before the show – said that he deserved a gold medal for that. Everyone laughed, and then they were done.

Nothing happened.

No, that's not true. Loads of things happened. Sixteen people called, saying they knew who Yeromy was and would tell them for a small fee. One psychic called and said Yeromy was in a better place. A few other radio stations called to interview Clara on the phone, and then it was quiet for two whole days, until the phone rang again.

"Are you ready?" Clara whispered to Yeromy. He winked back.

"I'm ready."

Clara opened the door quietly and stepped in.

"Gran?" she called. "Grandma?"

"Clara? Is that you? You're here early, lunch isn't for a few hours, is your father with you too? Come inside. You can peel the potatoes if you want. And Merry Christmas!"

"No, come out here," Clara called. "I've got your Christmas present."

"We usually open them after we've eaten, dear."

"But this one's already open. Just come, okay? Please? Just this once?" Clara heard Granny running the water.

"All right, all right, impatient girl, what is it you've..."

She was still drying her hands off on her apron when she spotted Yeromy in the hall.

"No... It can't... I've never... No, it can't be?" she said, covering her mouth with her hand and staring at Yeromy as if she'd seen a ghost.

"Grandma, this is Yeromy Okeke."

"No..." she whispered.

"He's the grandson of your Yeromy. And this is his father." Clara turned to Mr. Okeke.

"I'm so glad to meet you," he said. "My father told us all about you. He called you his best Christmas friend."

Grandma clutched the Christmas tree brooch, her eyes filled with water.

"You look just like him," she said to the boy called Yeromy. "It's as if 63 years went by and I was eight years old again. Just like him."

"Everyone says that," said Yeromy. Grandma sniffled.

"Well, come in! Come in! I'll pop the kettle on."

"I'm afraid we can't stay long, Mrs. Morgan," said Mr. Okeke.

"Oh, Ruth, please, call me Ruth," she said.

"Ruth," Mr. Okeke smiled. "That is my sister's name."

"It's a good name," Granny said. As no one was moving, she didn't seem to know what to do. "I'm sorry your father is no longer with us," she said.

"Oh! No, I'm sorry. Dad's fine! He moved to Australia many years ago. He's there now. But when we heard your story on the radio –" Grandma looked to Clara, who grinned. They hadn't told her anything about it yet. "– I knew right away that it had to be my father you were looking for. I sent him the clip, and he got so excited. He sent you this," said Mr. Okeke, and he pulled a small parcel out of his pocket.

"Dear Ruthie," Grandma read from the little card. "I

hear it's time for an upgrade. I hope to hear from you soon. Your best Christmas friend, Yeromy."

"Upgrade?" she said, sniffling again, and then she lifted the lid of the small parcel.

"Oh," she said. "Oh. Oh my."

It was a golden Christmas tree brooch with small, raised rows of tinsel and sparkling rhinestone baubles.

"He also wanted me to give you this," Mr. Okeke said and handed over three small photographs. There was a yellow post-it note on the top one, saying 'Every year'.

In the first picture was a young boy who indeed looked a lot like the Yeromy standing right there. The boy in the picture was smiling to the camera, hanging a beautiful ceramic dove on a Christmas tree.

In the second picture, a young man was holding a baby on one arm while hanging a bauble on the tree with the other. Right above the bauble was the bird.

The third picture showed a rather old man, smiling from a chair next to a Christmas tree. The dove had lost a bit of the right wing, but was otherwise hanging proudly on the tree.

"Every year," whispered Grandma. "Every, single year."

The gap between the Now and Then

His name was Eon Endless, and he lived on the small island right between Now and Then. On this island, he was the only inhabitant, and he liked to think of himself as the king.

"Good morning, Your Majesty," he would say to himself in the morning.

"Good morning, Your Highness," his mirror image would reply. This bothered Eon a little. 'Your Highness' is the way to address a prince, and he didn't like the thought of the miserable man in the mirror ranking higher than himself.

Eon Endless had a wonderful job. The tides of time ran past his island, carrying the Now into the Then, turning the present into the past. But every so often, for a brief moment or two, Eon Endless would raise the barrier of possibilities and a gap in time would occur. A split second in which people could – with the slimmest possible margin – escape an oncoming car, for example, or catch a full glass of milk falling from the counter. These were the moments where a penny would land on its edge, or someone could crunch up your crisp packet and make an impossible throw. Watch it glide through the air and land in the bin on the other side of the room – having gone straight over the head of the one you were trying to impress. These moments were known by many names – coincidences, miracles, magic or luck – but Eon himself called them gifts, and he dealt them out often and with great joy.

Time is a curious thing, however, and no matter what you turn it to, it will eventually break it down. Eon Endless had been king of his little island for thousands of years, never had a holiday or missed other people. But one day, everything changed. When he woke up and went to greet himself in the mirror, the only thing looking back at him was a lonely old man.

"Good morning…" he said, then sighed. There was no point to the 'Your Majesty' greeting. It was only the two of them there.

"What's wrong, Your Highness?" said his reflection.

"I'm lonely," Eon said. "I haven't spoken to anyone but you for so long I've forgotten what it feels like to have a difficult conversation, or to disagree with someone, or laugh." He sighed again. One of those long, deep sighs that lingers on the edge of a sob.

"Want me to tell you a joke?" said the reflection.

"Sure," said Eon Endless, thinking it was worth a try.

"It's a knock-knock joke," his reflection cautioned.

"That's okay," said Eon.

"Okay, you start," said his reflection, grinning a little.

"Knock knock," said Eon.

"Who's there?" said the reflection.

"… Ah." said Eon, and went outside, the mirror still laughing behind him.

Eon stood staring out over the ocean of time. He raised the invisible barrier and watched the gap in time stretch out like dry sand in front of him, then turned it back down after a second. He had done this so many times and never once questioned the point of it all, but now he could do nothing else. After an hour or so, when time came to raise it again, something new happened. Something that had never happened before. Eon Endless turned on the barrier, then left his post. The gap between the Now and Then grew, stretching out wider and wider in front of him. Eon Endless shrugged, and stepped in between the walls of ocean.

It was still a narrow gap. He had to step sideways, edging his way down the water-edged corridor. On one side, he had everything that ever happened, mixed and distorted through the glassy waves. On the other side he looked into the present – not just this present, but every present that had ever been. Everything that was currently happening somewhen stood frozen in a breathless moment, waiting for the wave to roll on into the past.

It was strange, he thought, how he had been staring down this gap all this time, but never wondered what was on the other side. Somewhere, out there, it surely had to open onto somewhere else, didn't it?

He chose not to think about the consequences this long a gap would have as it widened on either side of him. Usually, it was no more than a paper-thin hiccup in the flow of things. By now, he could have stretched his arms wide to either side and still not touched water with either hand.

The ground was dry, full of seashells and scurrying time crabs who didn't know to when they belonged. The deep ocean on either side and the ever-growing space between the Now and the Then made him feel like he was shrinking. He didn't mind the feeling at all. Something new, once in five thousand years. He kept walking.

"It can't be good," he heard from somewhere in front of him. "It's never done this before... Should we keep pouring possibilities into it? I mean... it's already a bit much, don't you think?"

"That's what we do," said another voice, shaky, breathy and uneven, as if spoken through an old, toothless mouth. "We pour in possibilities as long as the space is open. May not be good that it's taking this long, but gives us a chance to get rid of some island clutter." Hoarse, hissing laughter followed, and the sound of splashes in time.

"Hello?" said Eon. "Who's there?"

"Ah, I sense trouble now," said the shaking voice, but the other just scoffed.

"Don't be silly," it said, "It's just people. Hello? We're Sudden and Surprising Sometimes." The voice belonged to a woman. She sounded just as old as the other speaker, but warm and round and living. "Who's that?"

"I'm Eon Endless," he said.

"Are you now?" said the old man, "I'll be damned."

Around the bend, Eon Endless stepped onto another island, where an old couple were busy throwing possibilities into the Now.

"Are you... Do you... Are you the ones who make unlikely things happen?" Eon said.

"Could be," shrugged the lady. Then she stretched out her hand and smiled, "I'm Surprising," she said, "And this is my husband Sudden. This is the island of Could Be. I take it you come from the sister island?"

"I... I don't know," said Eon. "I make the gap between Now and Then."

"Some gap you've made today," said Sudden conversationally, as if he was commenting on nothing more peculiar than a bird flying above their heads.

"Yes... I just wanted to see if there was someone else out here," he said. "I'm lonely."

"Oh, dear," Surprising said, pressing her hand to her mouth. "Are you on your island all alone?"

"Yes," Eon said, looking at his feet.

"Oh, I couldn't do this without Surprising," Sudden shook his head. "Why haven't you had a partner sent?"

"I can have a partner?" Eon said. The old couple looked at each other, then shrugged.

"Could be," they both said.

Eon stayed for a cup of tea. They sat on the beach, watching the tremendous gap stretch and widen until they could see all the way over to Eon's island. Then a terrible sound tore through the air. It was the sound of a thousand bolts of lightning hitting a thousand pianos. A splintering crash with myriad lingering harmonics clinging to the air.

"Oh dear," said Surprising, staring at the sky and grabbing her husband's hand.

"Oh no," Eon whispered. Above them, a huge tear had opened between the clouds. The very fabric of reality had ripped apart above the gap.

"You best go home, son," said Sudden, "close the gap. Go!"

"Please hurry," said Surprising, shoving Eon back out into the sea.

"But I wanted company," he said, suddenly more scared of going home alone than of the whole of time falling apart.

"I'm sure you'll get some," the old woman said.

"At least it could be," the man agreed.

Eon ran. He ran as the gap of time filled with possibilities that ran out from the rift in the sky and crashed into the gap. It filled with sparkling lights and strange coincidences no one would ever truly believe.

Eon ran as two armies who had been shooting at each

other just hours before decided to lay down their weapons and celebrate together for the night. He ran as a man-made box of metal, with three fragile humans inside, orbited the moon for the very first time, connecting Earth to space. Eon ran as a pregnant woman and a weary man found shelter in a calm and warm stable, in a town that was filled to the brim with visitors. He ran as angels sang in the fields, and a number of prophecies came true. He ran as unexplained lights were observed in a forest in England, and as a black American president smiled while the senate passed a historical healthcare reform. Every Now was in flux, filling with impossible things.

He threw himself onto the beach and lowered the barrier of possibilities. He worried it might be too late. The Now and the Then crashed into each other, burying the endless possibilities, and drew them out in both directions. In the ocean, a clear, glittering line could be seen. A shimmering, sparkling line that occurred every year throughout time. It lay there as a concentration of miracles, magic, coincidence and luck. It was beautiful, it was eternal, and Eon Endless knew it was a big mistake.

He heard the deep footsteps of the creator in the sand. And then, Eon Endless fell asleep.

When he woke up, his little house was bustling with activity.

"Good morning, Your Majesty," said a red-cheeked lady, and she kissed him squarely on the mouth. She winked at him, as if this was a private joke, just between themselves.

"Good morning, my princess," he said, smiling a smile that came all the way to his eyes.

There was nothing left of the tropical island he had been on just a day before. Outside the window, nothing but ice and snow stretched out as far as the eye could see.

"Have your breakfast now," his wife said, rustling his

hair gently. "Surprising and Sudden are ready for the briefing, they've figured it all out, and this year, they think we'll set a new record." She shrugged. "Something about utilising string theory."

It came to him then, that it was all in his memories, the way everything had changed. The rift in time had made too many miracles, too many prophecies come true at once. The barrier of time would have to open more seldom. The developing team of the creator had sent in a thousand bug reports until they finally found a fix.

Eon Endless had a new job now. His job was to sprinkle love and Christmas cheer through a single gap between the Now and Then. The biggest one of the year. A few more could be opened on occasion. And he was to use these to gather materials, to find new workers, to give the Mrs a holiday and other necessary things. But this one was pure, as it was for nothing but miracles, and could stretch as long as it wanted, through this one, wonderful night.

Eon Endless finished his breakfast and got dressed in his fur-lined robes.

"Good morning, old man," he said to his reflection, and his reflection smiled back with earnest happiness, and Eon Endless laughed.

"Ho ho," he said, then grabbed his wife and twirled her around a couple of times.

In the workshop, Surprising and Sudden were standing in front of a billion parcels and a hundred happy elves.

"It's all ready for you," they said, "We've redesigned your sleigh, and the list is longer. We think you can hand out as many gifts as you want, as the bag will never empty, and your time from house to house will be near nothing in this year's gap."

He looked at them with tears in his eyes, hugged them and thanked them for all the work they had done.

"You ready?" said his wife, kissing his cheek. "The impossible night is here."

Silent night

A few flecks of snow were the first things he saw when the doors opened. They fell slowly, drifting this way and that, as if they hadn't quite decided where they wanted to land yet and felt they could take their time. The air smelled different than he remembered.

"Do you think," he said, as the warden and the guard went through the procedures, passing sheets of paper between themselves, "that the high walls of the courtyard somehow make the air smell different than the air out here?"

They took no notice of him. Few people ever did. Tom Robins spoke with a soft voice, hesitant and meek, more like the rustling of paper.

"All right, Mr. Robins," the warden said. "Here you are." Then he looked down the lane for a moment. "Did you arrange for someone to pick you up?"

"Yes, warden," said Mr. Robins. "My sister said she'd come."

He didn't know why he'd asked for his own suitcase. The few belongings he'd owned would have fit in a paper bag, and he had passed most of them on to the other boys of Ward 6. He had given his bible to Stinky, who'd pretended not to want it. And he'd given his comb and towel to Samuel, to square the last lines of their debt.

Now, he placed the suitcase in the thin layer of snow and sat himself down to wait.

"Good luck out there," said the warden, shaking his hand and getting ready to step back inside.

"Thank you, sir," said Mr. Robins. "Good luck in there, to you." He had nothing but respect for the warden, and had they both lived different lives, they might have been the best of friends.

Just as the guard went in through the door, the warden pulled a cigarette out of his shirt pocket.

"Merry Christmas, Tom," he said, and held out his lighter so Mr. Robins could have a light. But Mr. Robins just tucked the cigarette behind his ear and shook the warden's hand again.

"Merry Christmas, warden," he said, and then he was alone.

Sitting on his suitcase, he tried to get to grips with all of the unfamiliar feelings that were welling up inside him. He felt a clear sensation that the world was too big, that it lacked corners, edges and borders he could identify. If he had stood up and started walking, he could have walked for hours before someone told him to stop, and if he chose his paths well, no one ever would. And the air really was different. He took it in in deep gulps, opened his mouth wide and pulled it in with a rattling gasp. It stung in his lungs, smelled pure and fresh, and unfamiliar, he thought. Not like his air at all.

He enjoyed having a hat on his head again. He had

never been particularly into fashion, but he'd always felt that wearing a hat made even the shabbiest suit look more dapper. As it was Christmas Eve, the mayor had expected a media turnout for some of the days of many releases and had granted clothing requests with a slightly more generous hand than normal. And there really had been media. Mr. Robins and Samuel had stood in the window all day, watching as Shivvy, Edgar and the posh kid from Ward 4 were reunited with crying spouses, pregnant girlfriends and mothers who had waited for years to see their dear, darling boys again. But it was 5pm now. The journalists were home, stuffing the turkeys and kissing under mistletoe, and no one was there to celebrate Mr. Robins' release.

She honked the horn as she came up through the yard, and for a second, he could have sworn his mother was sat behind the wheel. Debbie's thin frame was hunched over, all too close to the steering wheel, clutching the ten-to-two position as if car safety was a bodily function, not a choice. When she pulled up, he could see her closing her eyes and taking a deep breath before stepping out of the car.

The longing for his mother intensified as Debbie – her apron still on under her coat and rollers still in her hair – smiled at him with that altogether too tired smile he knew like the back of his own hand.

"Merry Christmas," she said, giving him an awkward hug. "Do you need to get your things, or...?" She blushed, noticing his suitcase, but he didn't mind.

"I'm glad you came," he said. "It's nice to see you."

She nodded, and grabbed his case. She made the awkward jerking motion of someone who expects a heavier load than they're getting, and smiled apologetically as the suitcase half flew into the back of the car.

They drove in absolute silence, passing more people than Mr. Robins could remember ever having seen. They were milling around in patterns he didn't recognise. Carrying bags from shops he'd never heard of, wearing clothes in garish colours and hairdos that looked like accidents. No one was wearing a hat, he noticed. Just the occasional old man.

The city lights were different. When they stopped at a set of traffic lights, a young man zoomed past the car on a small plank of wood. It made a tremendous ruckus as it rolled across the cobbles, and it whirled a few whisks of snow up behind it. On his shoulder, he carried a large black record player – although the record itself was nowhere to be seen – blaring out unfamiliar music, the base notes shaking the car.

Debbie turned to look at him a couple of times, smiled stiffly, but didn't speak. Not until they passed the street where their father's shop had been.

"It's a Tesco Express now," she said. "A grocery store."

"Oh," he said. And although he had never really thought that the shop would still be there, not the way it used to be, it made him sad to think it was gone.

"And Anita Bridgewater's laundry, remember that? That's a bookies now. Nothing in the street is the same," she said.

"I guess not," he said. Then he swallowed. "43 years is a very long time. I guess nothing is the same, really."

"No..." she said. "I don't think anything is."

Her flat was small and musty, and the loveliest place Mr. Robins had been in 43 years.

"This is nice," he said. "It reminds me of home." She smiled at him then, took his coat and hat, and hung them up on a peg on the wall.

"Lots of this is from home," she said, showing him

around. "This lamp used to be by the fire, remember? These paintings hung in the drawing room. Do you remember this?" she asked, holding up the ivory monkeys – see no evil, hear no evil, speak no evil – and he felt them stir up a rush of memories.

"Oh..." he said, "they were from Zanzibar. Uncle Lucas brought them back, and mum thought they were too vulgar to be in the dining room so dad kept them in his office." He smiled.

"Uncle Lucas? I thought it was Uncle Adam," she said, frowning.

"Maybe it was," he said, because he really didn't know.

"This is fantastic," he said, pointing at the turkey with his fork. "This is so good. Just like mum's!"

"I'm glad you like it," she smiled. She had brushed her curls out now, but he still thought they were altogether too small and made her hair look like a poodle. She wore a huge red jumper with a tight golden belt, and gigantic hoop earrings with tinsel wrapped around them. He thought they looked ridiculous, but she had called them festive and he didn't want to argue. Not today. Not ever, if he could help it.

She'd made ginger nuts and bought some stollen slices. They drank ginger beer and watched cartoons on the telly. Colour. He had heard of it, of course, but this was the first time he'd seen it for himself. She laughed just as easily as she had when they were kids, and it felt liberating to laugh at something that wasn't a crude story told by crude men.

"I saw Theoline Hopkins the other day," Debbie said out of the blue.

"Oh?"

"Yeah, she works down Church Street now, in some lawyer's office."

"Is that so."

"Yes, her husband died. She's a widow, you know."

"Oh, right."

"She said you should come over for a cuppa when you were out," Debbie said, picking at the pillow in her lap.

"Oh."

"I got her number and everything."

"Thanks."

At nine that evening, they started talking about the funerals. Mum's first, then Dad's. Mr. Robins hadn't been given leave to go to either.

"Everyone said," Debbie sniffed, "that you should have been allowed to go to your own mother's funeral. It's cruel and unusual punishment if not. But we tried so hard, and they wouldn't let you."

"It's okay," he said, "I've made peace with it. But thank you for taking pictures. It's nice.... It's nice to know they got a proper send off."

At nine thirty, they looked through the photo albums and talked about their childhood. At nine fifty-five, Debbie suddenly looked at the clock and grinned.

"I've got you something for Christmas," she said. "But you have to come here and sit in the chair. When the phone rings at ten, you've got to answer. Okay?"

"Okay."

Debbie left the room. Closed the door halfway behind her as if to signify that this was a private moment she wasn't part of, even though it was happening in her own house. At exactly ten o'clock, the phone chirped. The sound surprised him, as he was used to phones going *rrrrrring rrrrrring*. This one went *beepibee bee beep*, which is a different sound all together.

"Hello?" he said, enjoying the unfamiliar weight of the phone in his hand, the feeling of the twisted cable between his fingers. The phone was small, and lighter than the old one his parents used to have.

"Tom? Is that you?" said the voice of an old man.

"Yes... This is Tom."

"Now, I'll be damned. So they really did let you out in the end, huh?"

"Yes," said Mr. Robins, feeling he was stating the opposite.

"It's me, Tom," said the voice on the other end. "Rudy."

"Rudy!"

"So nice to know you're out here among us, old pal," Rudy said. "You'll never know where I am now."

"London?" Mr. Robins guessed.

"California! Land of raisins and pensioners."

"The US! That's... Wow. How you been, Rudy?"

"Oh you know. It's been a few... a bit of this, a bit of that. I'm married now. Got two little'ns just a few years after you went in. They're all grown now, of course. Expecting to be a grandpa soon."

"Grandpa Rudy," said Mr. Robins, a slight thickness to his voice that he couldn't quite explain.

"Yeah..." said Rudy.

They spoke for fifteen minutes. Rudy, mostly. After all, there hadn't been much to report about in the last 43 years from this side of the call. When they hung up, Rudy promised to call again in a day or two, and they agreed to meet up when the family came to visit next summer.

"I would invite you to come over here, of course," Rudy said, "but I guess you won't get a visa now."

"I don't know," Mr. Robins said. "Probably not."

Debbie was doing the dishes when he left the room. The radio was on, singing songs he didn't recognise.

"So, tomorrow," Debbie said, "Jackie's invited us over for Christmas lunch."

"Jackie?"

"Cousin Jackie. Uncle Adam's Jackie."

"Oh. Right," said Mr. Robins. He tried to mentally go through the list of cousins, but he couldn't remember a single one of their names. Somehow, his memory of extended family had gone. He remembered cousin Alfie, of course, because he had visited him a couple of times, but the rest were bland faces in an endless sea of memory.

"And in the evening, I thought we could go down to Bangers and meet up with Gus, Bob and Gillian. They're all still around," she said. "If you want."

"Sure," he said, drying off a plate that brought back memories of bananas and custard in his parents' house, and fresh bread with thick syrup from the 10-litre bucket they had kept in the pantry. "Sounds nice."

He turned to his sister, looking serious. "Thank you for letting me stay with you," he said, holding a saucer motionless in his hand. "It... It really means a lot." He took a step forward to hug her, again struck by how much she looked like their mother.

'Silent Night' played on the radio, so achingly familiar that Mr. Robins couldn't help a few tears escaping down the highway of his cheeks.

"You turning soft on me," Debbie said, staring at him with a grim look.

"Of course not," he said, wiping the tears away, although the song kept forcing new ones out of his eyes.

"You've got something on your shirt there," Debbie said, pointing somewhere right below his chest. He bent forward, only for Debbie to flick his nose.

"Ha ha, made you look!" she said, because some things never change.

The little graveyard behind the old church

The little graveyard behind the old church is a popular spot for evening walks and people showing others around. It's a beautiful place. It's quiet. Serene. The pond is home to happy frogs and a lonely swan that glides across the water without ever bothering visitors. The village has named him Swanson, and they gladly give him bread when they pass.

The myth is as old as the graveyard, or so the elders say. Swanson fell in love with the marble swan on Agatha Mirabelle Harris (1797–1805, The voice of an angel, never forgotten)'s grave, they say, and has stayed to guard it ever since. Mrs. Jacobs, who's 86 now, says Swanson was there when *she* was a child and that the pond has never frozen over. No one believes it, but they all know it's true.

The graveyard is a place for living. No one's been buried there for more than 200 years, so none of the visitors are there for the dead. And yet, they love the little graveyard behind the old church. It's a village secret. It's the village's pride.

But no one goes there at Christmas. If you asked them why not, the villagers would look at each other, shrug and maybe giggle.

"Just doesn't seem right," they'd say, and no matter how hard you pushed, you wouldn't find another reason hidden beneath the first.

Madame Augustine (whose real name is Doris Jenkins) says the aura of the graveyard changes on Christmas Eve. She says a psychic shield goes up, and then, even she (the most sensitive psychic this side of the Thames) struggles to remember that the graveyard exists. She's wrong of course – there's no such thing as a psychic shield. It's nothing more than a little magic. Christmas magic, if you want particulars.

On Christmas Eve, around 8pm, Swanson stretches his long neck and looks to the marble swan. And, though you wouldn't believe it if you didn't see it yourself, the marble swan turns its head and looks back at him, with such tenderness that you'd swear she, too, is in love.

Swanson leaves the pond, then – the only time a year, if you believe the rumours – and waddles up past the graves of Captain Morris Williams (1678–1731, Deeply admired and sorely missed) and his wife Mrs. Captain Morris Williams née Lucas (1688–1733, Beloved wife and mother).

Only when the marble swan jumps down to greet her love does the little ghost girl spring out of the ground. She stretches and laughs and cartwheels in the air before beginning her round to wake the others.

Come mothers come fathers
Come villagers all

It is time, it is time
For our Christmas ball
Come grandmothers, cobblers
Come Captain and wife
Come dance through the night
Like we once danced through life
Come grandfather Willows
Come organist Young
It is time, it is time
For a Christmas song

She chants her verses as she jumps from grave to grave, calling out their names and helping them brush dirt off their forms when they rise. Each of them stretches and yawns. They greet each other like old friends. The captain and his wife embrace for a long time, and sometimes sneak a kiss, if they think no one's watching.

Come snowflakes and starlight
Come crystals of ice
Our winter-cold graveyard
A fool's paradise

The chant has many verses, and they've heard them so many times before that when the initial greetings are over, they join in the chanting while Agatha jumps. The chant tells their stories, mentions them all by name. It even mentions the man buried right outside the grounds, and the sad story of his wrongful execution. He often shows up a little late, seemingly a bit uncomfortable with the whole event.

Seamlessly, without anyone wondering how or why, the chant glides into the first of many songs. Merchant Peterson (1840–1888, rest in peace) holds the ghostly memory of his fiddle, and plays for them all to dance.

Organist Young's voice keeps them all to the right verses and fills in the lyrics if the others forget. The Captain and his wife dance every dance for the first few hours; then they walk – hand in hand – down to the pond to chat.

This is the pattern they all follow. At first, they dance and sing, laugh and play in the ghost light. But sooner or later, they all fall into conversations with their loved ones, old friend and neighbours – or even just friends from the last 200 years of Christmas celebrations. It is a night of endless love.

When the first little strip of daylight touches the sky, Agatha climbs down from her mother's lap and claps her hands in a new beat.

Friends and beloved of old church grounds
Another year's dancing on burial mounds
One night of Christmas for all ghosts to share
Dancing and loving
Singing and chanting
Now, to all, Merry Christmas and a Happy New Year

This is a song. It is simple and strange in its dragging rhythm and surprising tune, but it calls them all back to the graveyard, and begins the process of goodnight. They all hug and say their goodbyes, sinking slowly into their graves and returning to their deep sleep. They will rest now, until the next year's Christmas ball comes around.

The Captain and his wife sink through the earth while giving each other one last kiss, and soon, the graveyard is nothing but a graveyard. Agatha's mother waits by her grave for her daughter to finish the last few verses.

"You take care, now, dear girl," she says, straightening Agatha's translucent shawl on her non-corporeal body. "And stay as warm as you can. I love you very much." She gives her daughter a hug and a kiss on the cheek.

"I love you too, mammy," Agatha says as her mother disappears.

"Merry Christmas," Agatha whispers to the marble swan. She's stepping through the night with Swanson by her side, and as Agatha's dark locks disappear into the mold, the swan returns to its plinth and is once again nothing but stone.

Swanson will squawk, but only once. It may sound sad, but if you knew him, you would hear that it's a sound of gratitude and joy. Knowing, as he does, that it's only a year until next year. And a year passes terribly fast when you're endless.

The little graveyard behind the church is a wonderful place. It is loved by the villagers and the love has seeped through the grounds. But no one goes there at Christmas. And that may be just as well.

What happens on the top of things

The rooftops, tiles, the top of things. That's where the wild ones live. Even when it's freezing, even when the city is covered in thick, wet snow, they scramble barefoot across the houses. Above the city. Out of sight from the constable and his truncheon, out of sight from the rich folks with their ideas of clean streets, and out of sight from the poor folks who dole out coppers and beatings in equal measure. Up here, the children rule.

The children, and Master Smoke, of course. They say he used to be a sweeper, a sweeper who simply forgot how to get down. Now, he lives between the two chimneys above the baker's shop. It's warm there all year round. And dry enough, as long as he stays under his canvas cover.

He waxes it, they say, with beeswax he finds in the hives beneath the gables.

"Wait for me," says Little Pop, falling behind as the big boys run. He coughs and has to stop for air. He's had a cold for weeks.

"Keep up, slowpoke," says Dagger. He's got a soft spot for the youngest, although he'd never say. Rumour says the two are brothers, but no one knows for sure. They ended up on the top of things, one in the spring and another in winter, several years apart. But Dagger thinks he remembers a baby with a scarlet scar. And Pop – who runs with a scarlet scar – thinks he remembers a brother, before the rent got too expensive, and the woman packed up the toddler and left the other one behind. Dagger hangs back, lets the kid catch up, worries over his shiny eyes and blushing cheeks. But not for too long. Everyone gets ill on the top of things.

They step and slide across the roofs, tiles clattering under their feet.

"It's almost time!" someone calls, and they speed up, leap across the narrow lanes, staying clear of the wider streets. The setting sun dyes the snow pink and purple. It's a beautiful night for a feast.

Someone has made a bridge. They do this every year. A bridge from the baker's shop to the big flat roof of the Temple. One after the other, they scurry across. Find their places in front of Master Smoke. He's waiting for them. Smiling, like no one else in their lives. He frowns when Little Pop coughs his rattling cough, like no one else will (not even Dagger).

From all over town, the wild ones appear. There are 30 or so, maybe 40. No one counts, as they don't want to know. The southside clan and the northside clan would normally not cross paths like this, but it's the winter festival, and Master Smoke belongs to everyone.

"Once upon a different time," he says when they've all settled down. He speaks very quietly, makes sure no one down in the real world will hear, "there was a young maid who was employed by the King."

Little Pop shivers, his scraps can't keep the deep chill of the snow from his bones. Dagger edges closer to him, his body like a furnace for the youngster.

"The maid had only one job," Master Smoke continues, "and that was to look after an old sword. The sword was kept in the tallest tower, inside three locked chests, behind three locked doors. Every day, the maid unlocked the three doors and the three chests and polished the sword for three hours. Then she placed it back inside three chests and made her way through three doors, locking them firmly behind her."

The wild ones are listening closely. Master Smoke has brought – bought or stolen – stacks of loaves and blankets. They share the bread between them and hand out blankets to those who need them the most. There aren't enough (there never are), but Dagger makes sure Little Pop gets one; he always has one tucked away for himself in a very safe place. He wraps this new blanket around Little Pop's shoulders, and no one dares tease him, as Master Smokes is strict about these things, and they don't want the story to end.

"At first, the maid thought there had to be magic in the sword. Why else would the King keep it so well protected? But no matter how many times she returned, it never made anything happen.

"It was a big job. Hours and hours she spent locking and unlocking, polishing and replacing. Years passed by, but the King insisted she keep up with the task, and he paid her handsomely to do so. Her hair went from black to steel, and finally she was as white as snow, still polishing the sword every day.

"'My Lord,' she said one day, kneeling in front of the King. 'I'm afraid the sword is gone.'

"'What?' the King shouted, so angry the maid felt her mouth glue shut with fear for a second.

"'I'm sorry,' she said, tears running down her old cheeks, 'I've been polishing the sword for fifty-one years, and now there's nothing left. I wore through the blade a few years ago now, the grip went early last spring. The pummel lasted until today, but now there's nothing but dust.'

"'Why didn't you stop?' the King screamed. 'Why didn't you tell me you were wearing it down?'

"'My Lord,' said the maid, staring at her feet, 'what did you think would happen?'"

All the bread is gone now, even the crumbs (even the ones that fell in the snow). The children sit huddled together, enthralled by the many voices of Master Smoke. Little Pop is resting his head gently on Dagger's shoulder. The winter festival makes him brave, and he dares reach for this moment of intimacy, safe in the knowledge that no one will notice. Not even Dagger. The story has swallowed him too.

"The King was furious. The sword had been his most valuable possession, an heirloom from some distant forefather who won it in some distant war.

"He opened the three locked doors, ran to open his three locked chests, and there – in the bottom – was a pile of steel shavings, resembling nothing but dust being dust. In anger, the King had the maid thrown into a dark dungeon, deep under three mountains, across three endless seas.

"For days, the maid cried. There was just a single opening in her dungeon, a small tunnel stretching straight up through the mountain. The hole so deep she could only ever see stars through the opening. So deep it was. So dark it was. But the world is a mysterious place," Master Smoke says, making sparks spring from his hands, making the children jump with surprise.

"There is magic in the air, and there is magic in people." The sparks dance around the children, who laugh and try to catch them with their hands.

"A snowstorm raged on the mountain above, and a flurry got lost and hurtled down through the tunnel. The maid, now tired of crying, caught the flurry of snow by its tail, beat it flat and wove it into a polishing cloth. The cloth remembered being snow, and the snow remembered being water, and the water remembered being an ocean, and that was all she would ever need.

"Every day, she stretched her arms thrice, and every evening she bent her legs thrice. The rest of the day, she polished away on the wall in her dungeon, knowing deep in her heart that a mountain is softer than a sword of steel, and an ocean is stronger than a mountain, too.

"What can we learn, lads and lassies, from the maid in her hole and the King?"

The kids lean in, eager for the lesson. None of them – except possibly Princess, but she's a liar – has ever gone to school, but this is the next best thing. Master Smoke's lessons are big and complicated, but they've come in handy more than once. Little Pop coughs again, and Dagger knocks his back a couple of times, helping to break up what's stuck in his chest.

"One!" Master Smoke says, holding a finger to the sky. "What you prize the most should be shown and shared. If you keep it too close, it may crumble to dust." He smiles at them all, as if any of them owns anything more than a blanket hidden in a very safe place. "Two!" he continues. "Most of our lives, we do things that are pointless and hard. But that hardens us too. And when we are hard, we can survive. And when we survive, we can find joy," he says, allowing the sparks to form a big star above his head, glowing tendrils reaching out and around them, tickling their noses and making them laugh.

"And three," he says, opening a bag by his feet and pulling out the most wonderful oranges. They're barely mouldy at all, many of them not even soft. "We must never give up, but keep trying. You never know when a solution will present itself."

There's an orange for everyone. Dagger trades his with Little Pop's on inspection – the little one's probably never had one before, and he deserves to start with as little mould as possible. Dagger watches him eat, then gives him half of his own orange, too. He's heard oranges are good against colds.

Then they all leave. The southside clan leaves first, not looking back as they return to the docks, out of this rivalling turf. Then the northside clan leaves. They move slowly, filled with laughter and joy. Some of them help Master Smoke back to his chimneys. Some help the youngest get back off the roof. Dagger puts his arm around Little Pop's shoulder, thinking about the King's sword, and dust. He's kept his spot hidden for a very long time. He never gets to use his blanket, he's too worried that someone will see him and steal it. But the little one's ill, and could use it. And he could use the warmth from the chimney back there, and the bottle of cough syrup Dagger's kept out of sight.

"I've got something to show you," he says, sucking sweet juice from the last wedge of his orange. "It's a very safe place where I keep my blanket. It has a nice warm place to sleep, and some medicine I stole last year. You can have some. And you can keep your blanket there too, if you wish." Little Pop coughs and takes Dagger's hands.

They're probably not brothers, but they are, nonetheless.

The winter festival continues below, the spired city's many musicians weaving out into the streets to sing through the night. But up here, on the rooftops, the tiles, on the top of things, the night sings its own songs that only the wild ones can hear.

Christmas reprogrammed

The robot didn't, strictly speaking, *need* to have a face. So far, it had only had the signalling lights, the speakers and the output printer. But with a few buttons, some paper and a bottle of super glue, Mr. Jenkins managed to turn that into a passably nice face. The output printer made a nice mouth, the speakers gave it rosy cheeks and the signalling lights gave it three little eyes – two of which Mr. Jenkins gave eyebrows, hoping the children would let the third eye pass. He glued a big red button on as a nose and added a few more along the edge of the machine – not for any particular reason, just because he got carried away.

He had promised them, even *sworn*, that he wouldn't need to work over Christmas. But project AF-G7 hadn't gone as smoothly as planned, and if everything was to be ready for the New Year's presentation, he simply couldn't see another way.

"G7?" he said when he was done.

"Yes?" said the robot. Its voice was much smoother since they'd found the new voice profile output. It sounded almost real. Mr. Jenkins didn't like it – it was too calm. Eerily serene, he thought. It reminded him of the condescending wheatgrass-eating yoga teacher his wife had introduced him to. Calm and smiling all the time.

"I'm taking you home for Christmas. My family will be there. So... I need you to have a name."

"My name is G7," said the machine helpfully. Mr. Jenkins sighed.

"I know, but for the next few days, I need you to have a normal human name."

"Maria is a very normal human name," concluded G7.

"I think it should be a male one."

"John is a very common male human name."

"My name is John," said Mr. Jenkins, fighting the need to defend his name. It *was* very common, after all. "I think we should have different names. How about Derrick?"

"Derrick is a male human name."

"Derrick it is."

Mr. Jenkins couldn't put his finger on why, but he felt the robot was displeased. As if it was being quiet not because it hadn't been asked to say anything, but because it was making a point.

"Do you not... *like* the name Derrick?" Mr. Jenkins said, scolding himself for being silly. Mr. Jenkins hated being silly.

"I have no concept of 'like'. But I do not believe the name fits my programmed persona," said the robot.

"O... kay...?" said Mr. Jenkins, packing up the last of his papers. "What name would you like, then?"

"I believe Alfred is the superior name," said the robot.

Mr. Jenkins stared at it. "Alfred it is," he said. He shoved the rest of his notes into his suitcase and got ready to lift G7 – or Alfred – off the table.

"I can call you Betty," it said suddenly.

"What? No. You call me Mr. Jenkins," Mr. Jenkins said.

"And Betty, when you call me, you can call me Al."

"What?"

"Ha. Ha," said the robot. Then it turned on its speakers and played Paul Simon's 'You Can Call Me Al' at full volume. Mr. Jenkins turned down the volume and frowned.

"I don't think you should be able to do that," he said.

"Sending bug report," G7 said, and it printed the receipts through its mouth.

It was strange, Mr. Jenkins thought later, how quickly he had actually come to think of the output printer as its mouth and the signalling lights as its eyes. When he placed it in the car boot, he couldn't make himself shut the lid. He stared down on the stupid little face, and it looked back at him with its stupid raised eyebrows. As if sending him a sarcastic gaze.

"So this is what you're doing, is it? Locking people in the boot of your car and just letting them stay in the darkness? I see, so that's what you do," its face said, and Mr. Jenkins hated it.

"You're not real," he said and slammed the boot door shut. He could hear G7 arguing over semantics through the door, but tried to ignore it.

The house oozed Christmas. Every window had lights in it and both doors held beautiful wreaths. There were glowing reindeer on the lawn, blinking icicles hanging from the gutters; the great spruce was covered in tiny twinkling lights. Through the kitchen window, Mr. Jenkins could see his wife at the counter, finishing off dinner, perhaps, or baking another variation of Christmas cookies. He could tell she was singing. Probably 'Have Yourself a Merry Little Christmas'. It seemed to have been on her mind for days. He sighed, adjusted the eyebrows on G7 and stepped inside.

"I'm home!" he called, hanging his hat on the hook by the door and shaking snow off his coat.

"Daddy!" the kids called, and came running out to greet him. They spotted G7 and skidded to a halt.

"Hello, honey, how was –?" Christina said, then she, too, froze.

"Kids, honey… this is Alfred. Say hello, Alfred."

"Hello."

"Hello," little Tina said shyly.

"Is that *work*?" said David, his eyes much darker than an eight-year-old's should be.

"Well… it's… *He's* from work, but I just…"

"You *promised*," said David, and her turned and ran up the stairs. Tina, not sure what to think of the situation, looked after her brother, then to the robot.

"Pommised," she said, and followed her brother up the stairs.

Mr. Jenkins looked up. "Honey, I…" he tried, but his wife held her hands up and shook her head.

"I can't even…" she said, and disappeared back into the kitchen.

"I sense that didn't go to well," G7 said. "My protocols suggest a swift apology, flowers and chocolates. I believe these are all applicable to the circumstance. Would you like me to order some for you?"

"What? No," Mr. Jenkins said.

"Yes!" his wife called from the kitchen.

"… Okay. Yes, please," Mr. Jenkins mumbled.

"I'm on it!" said G7, with altogether too much cheer.

Mr. Jenkins tried. He tried to apologise to his wife and kids. He tried to finish his work as quickly as he could; he tried to work all night so he could be present during the day. But he failed in all regards. Come Christmas Eve, David and Tina had come to loathe the robot in the office.

"I promise," Mr. Jenkins said, "I won't work tomorrow." He thought about it. "Well... I won't work in the morning, so we can open presents and have breakfast together. But maybe I could have a few hours before lu–" his wife shot him an incredulous look. "No, not before lunch, but maybe before Granny and Grandpa come for dinner?"

"But that's when we watch cartoons!"

"I know, Danny, but this is very important... If I can't figure this out before New Year's, I won't get... I may lose..." There was no way to finish the sentence and keep the Christmas calm, he realised.

"I'm sorry," he said. "I'll try not to work at all tomorrow... until after dinner, at least."

"You promised you wouldn't work over Christmas at *all*," Daniel mumbled into his hot chocolate.

"Pommised!" said Tina, holding her pinky in the air.

It was 1.30am before Mr. Jenkins went to bed that night. His wife had filled the stockings and placed the presents under the tree, and he just remembered to take a couple of bites out of the cookies and drink a little of the milk before stepping onto the stairs.

"Santa?" called Daniel from the top floor. Mr. Jenkins could just make out his son in the darkness. He was wearing dinosaur pyjamas and rubbing sleep out of his eyes. Mr.

Jenkins stepped back into the shadow and shifted into the kitchen. He was too tired to ruin his son's faith in Santa or get into another argument about work. He heard his son step down the stairs, and prayed he wouldn't insist on starting Christmas morning this early. As soon as he saw the slight form disappear into the living room, Mr. Jenkins hurried up the stairs, slipped under the covers, and promised himself he'd be a better father in the new year.

Daniel Jenkins approached the robot with a hammer in his right hand and a firm grip around Mister Miggles' fluffy right arm. He had checked the living room – Santa had already been there. Whatever Daniel and Mister Miggles got up to tonight, it wouldn't count towards being naughty until *next* Christmas. Daniel figured that if he was just really, really good for the rest of the year – really, *really* good – whatever he did tonight wouldn't matter.

He wished Dad hadn't glued that stupid face on it. It made this a little harder. But only a little.

"Stupid robot," he said, and he banged it hard right between the lights.

"My name is Alfred, how may I help you?" said the robot, a chipper twinge in its voice. Daniel slammed the hammer down again, this time knocking off the button nose.

"I believe you are trying to harm my hardware," the robot said, "and I must inform you that an emergency protocol will be activated should the attack persist."

Daniel didn't know what that meant, but it didn't sound good.

"But I need you to turn off!" he said, wrapping Mister Miggles up under his arm for moral support.

"You are not authorised to issue that command," said the robot. Then its light flickered a couple of times, and it continued. "May I enquire why you want me to initiate shut down?"

"'Cause you're ruining Christmas," said Daniel.

The robot was quiet for a bit. "I'm sorry, your statement has been deemed nonsensical."

"You're nonsensical," said Daniel.

"Agree to disagree," said the robot.

"Shut up!"

The robot went quiet. Daniel felt the weight of the hammer in his hand and wondered what would happen if he kept hitting.

"Can't you just turn off until after Christmas?" he said. "Please?"

"Whatever for?"

"Because I don't want you to ruin it!"

"I have no interest in ruining Christmas, nor do I believe I have the ability to."

"Yes, you do!" said Daniel, and although he could have sworn he was just angry, tears had started sloshing out of his eyes.

"Please hold," said the robot, and Daniel waited.

"Do I stop the Christian celebration of the birth of the improbable Baby Jesus all over the world?"

"No?"

"Do I keep turkey and cranberry sauce from making it to the dinner table?"

"No?"

"Do I somehow interfere with the decorations or the presents?"

"No!"

"Then, according to my database, I have no impact on Christmas whatsoever," said the robot, and it sounded so reassuring, as if it had solved a problem.

"You know," said Daniel, wiping away tears, "Dad always says how intelligent you are, but you're not! You're super dumb!"

"Was my conclusion incorrect? Should I rerun the algorithm?"

"You won't get it," Daniel said. "Christmas isn't like that."

The robot went quiet again, but the lights were blinking and shifting, as if it was in deep thought. "My programming suggests to me that you may wish to explain what Christmas is in your own limited understanding," said the robot.

"I don't know that I can," said Daniel, "'cause not all of it is like... things. It's Christmas when we get up too early to open the presents, and mum keeps falling asleep against dad's shoulder, but pretends that she's not. And it's Christmas when we get hot chocolate for breakfast, and I can put extra marshmallows on it, and no one minds. And Dad winks at me, and then he does the dishes while mum reads a weird book with Christmas decorations and people kissing on the cover. And then we play board games until lunch, and Dad sometimes lets us win, and this year, Tina will be old enough to play, maybe. I got her a game for Christmas, you know. One that's made for babies. And then we have lunch with Auntie Helen and Uncle George, and Auntie Helen opens Christmas crackers with me, and Dad laughs at all the jokes. And when they leave, I get to sit with Dad on the couch and watch cartoons for a long time. They're the same ones we watch every year, but they're nice, and they *feel* Christmassy. You know?"

The robot blinked a few times. "No, I'm sorry Mister Daniel, I do not know."

"But you're ruining it!" Daniel continued, "'cause Dad's

working *all* the time, and he's only thinking about you."

Again, they both went quiet, the robot thinking away and Daniel cuddling Mister Miggles.

"I am work," said the robot.

"Yes," said Daniel.

"How long is Christmas?"

"A few days," said Daniel, "at least, Christmas Eve – which you've already ruined – Christmas and Boxing Day."

"Three days, then," said the robot. His eyes blinked twice, and a small piece of card pushed out through its mouth. Then he went dark.

"Thanks, Alfred," whispered Daniel, and he ran off to bed.

The robot waited a few minutes, listening to sounds in the house. When he was satisfied that everyone was asleep, G7 – Alfred – went to work.

Mr. Jenkins snuck out of bed after a few hours of sleep. He hurried downstairs, eager to put in a few hours of work before the family got up. His office was flooded with paper. Everywhere he looked, bounds and bounds of G7's narrow paper strips lay folded in loops and bounds.

"No, no, no, no, no," he moaned, wading through the sea of paper until he got to the robot. He tore the end of the paper out of its mouth and read the last few lines.

...which, in conclusion, should solve the problem. I have therefore initiated a three-day reset protocol.

"What?!" Mr. Jenkins said, folding up the paper, skimming the length of code. There were calculations – long and intricate ones. In some places, individual pieces were framed and commented on, the robot slowly elaborating on the problem Mr. Jenkins had been working so hard to solve.

"G7?" he said, "G7 can you hear me? Alfred!"

He pushed the buttons, twiddled the dials, but the robot seemed to be nothing but a metal box. He felt like screaming. What could he do? He'd have to take the robot into the office, take it apart, run diagnostics... it would take the rest of Christmas to get this sorted. Unless...

He pulled until he found the beginning of the paper strip, read through it closely. It took him an hour and a half to understand it. It was his own code, and at first he thought that was all there was. That Alfred had printed out his entire code string for no good reason. But then he found a change. A small change, but a significant one.

This can't be right, Mr. Jenkins thought, then looked even closer. There were a few changes – suggestions for a new rebooting system that would fix the current bugs without... *But what about the algorithm duplicator?* Mr. Jenkins looked closer, reading each string of code, every calculation with deep concentration.

"Now, I'll be damned," he said. This could actually work. The robot seemed to have written itself a programme that would fix the whole issue. It shouldn't be able to do that. And it certainly shouldn't be able to initiate its own reboot. But even so...

"This could work," he mumbled. "This could actually work!" He didn't know if what he was feeling was relief or terror, but this was as good a shot as any. He would give the robot its three days, and see what it came up with. At least now he wouldn't have to work at Christmas. There was a beep. Then another. A single card came through the robot's mouth.

MERRY CHRISTMAS, BETTY. XX it said. Mr. Jenkins heard the first tip-taps of eager children's feet atop the stairs. They were coming down for stockings and breakfast. Mr. Jenkins smiled.

"Merry Christmas, Al..." he said, and he closed the office door behind him as he left.

Helping others to help ourselves

Early in December, the doorbell at Sunset Escapes swung happily from side to side and a fresh gust of air swept through the room. Annabelle looked up, but although the door had definitely opened, no one had entered the shop. She shrugged and went back to work, glad for the moment's distraction.

"'Scuse me," said someone in front of her. Leaning forward, she could just about spot the brown locks of a small child, not even reaching the top of her tall desk.

"Oh, hello sweetheart! What's your name?" said Annabelle, wheeling her chair to the side of her desk to see better. It was a girl, five, maybe six years old and smiling an oddly tight-lipped smile for such a young face. She looked familiar, but Annabelle couldn't quite place her.

"I'm Heloise," the child said, "and I want to buy a holiday, please."

"Is your mum or dad coming with you?"

"No, just my mum is going."

"All right, we'll wait for her then, shall we?"

The child looked troubled. Her face serious. "No, it's a surprise," she said eventually. "I want to buy a holiday for mammy. It's for Christmas!" She smiled a smile of relief, as if she'd finally found a way to express a difficult concept.

"I see," Annabelle said, smiling. "That's a very good Christmas present. Isn't it? Does your mum know you're here, sweetheart?"

"No, 'cause it's going to be a surprise," the girl said patiently.

"All right. Where's your mother now?"

Heloise looked at her, her eyes darting out the window, worry creeping over her face. "Can I please buy a holiday please?" she said, taking a step away from the desk.

"Holidays are very expensive, honey. I think it's best if we let your mum know you're here so she doesn't get worried. Don't you?"

The child backed towards the door, her eyes wild and white, like those of a frightened horse. "You mustn't tell!" she said. "It's a surprise, I want her to be happy."

"I'm sorry," Annabelle said, trying to put on her most reassuring face, "I didn't mean to startle you. You look cold, do you want some hot chocolate?"

Heloise looked at her, a slight suspicion across her face.

"Buying a holiday takes a little time, you see, so we usually ask our customers if they want a tea or coffee. But I think," she said, leaning forward and lowering her voice, "since you're the only customer here, that we can be a little naughty and have hot chocolate instead. Don't you?" She winked.

"Okay!" said Heloise, more at ease now.

"Do you want to sit down in one of those chairs and we can find out what sort of holiday your mum wants?"

Annabelle watched as the little girl climbed into the chair, knee first.

"Ollie!" she called. "Could you bring two hot chocolates please?"

"With you in a minute!" Ollie called from the back office.

"So, what kind of holiday does your mum want, do you think?"

"One where I'm not coming," Heloise said seriously.

"Oh, I'm sure that's not true..." Annabelle said. "Why do you say that?" She wrote a quick note for Ollie, pretending to take notes. *Call the police from the back office, keep your voice low, her name is Heloise, her mum doesn't know she's here.*

"She cries in the evening, sometimes," Heloise said, "and when we play, she always says she loves me but needs a holiday. She's very sad these days." Annabelle swallowed.

"Where's your dad, Heloise? Won't he be coming on the holiday?"

"No," Heloise says, "he's in Slough. He only comes at my birthday, sometimes. He has a horse and two more girls and a lady called Carol and a dog."

"I see," said Annabelle. Ollie came in with their hot chocolates.

"Ollie, this is Heloise," she said, reaching out to grab the hot chocolate from him. Without really thinking, she turned the note face down on the desk. *I'll give it a moment*, she reasoned. *Make sure I understand.* "Heloise wants to buy a holiday for her mum, who's very sad in the evenings and cries a lot," she said to Ollie. They exchanged glances, and he put a hand on Annabelle's shoulder.

"That sounds really hard," he said, pulling a chair over. "It must make you sad when your mum's sad."

Heloise nodded, blowing carefully at her hot chocolate

before taking a sip.

"You know," Ollie said, "our mummy used to be very sad in the evenings, too." The girl looked at them, but didn't respond. "We used to think it was our fault, but it really wasn't. It's just what happens to adults sometimes."

"Mammy's sad because granny died," said Heloise. "They had a big fight and then granny got too old to live any longer."

"Oh, that's very sad. Everyone gets sad when grand-mothers die. When did that happen?"

"In the summer," Heloise said, "But they fighted before I was born."

"That's a long time to be fighting."

"Yes. They didn't say sorry or anything." Heloise rolled her eyes.

"Heloise," Annabelle said, "what does your mum do? What's her job?"

"She fixes people's feet."

"Like, with massages and such?"

"No, in the hospital. With a saw, sometimes."

"That's a very good job," Annabelle smiled.

"Feet are the most important part of the body because they hold the rest of it up," the girl explained.

"That's very true," said Ollie, smiling, "Where is she right now, then?"

"She's sleeping."

"And did you make your way *all* the way here on your own? With a bus, maybe?"

"No..." said Heloise, cautious again.

"Do you live nearby, so you could walk?"

"You mustn't tell..." the girl said again, her mug frozen between her lap and her mouth.

"Oh, we won't tell," Ollie said easily." We just need to know so we can put the right names and addresses on the airplane tickets."

Annabelle sent a silent thanks to her older brother, always the clever one.

"We live there," Heloise said, pointing to the apartment above the butcher across the street.

"Oh! I've seen you in the window!" Annabelle said, realisation dawning. "You sometimes have a princess crown on, don't you?"

"It's a fairy crown..." Heloise said carefully. "It has glitter."

"Oh, I see – I've only seen it from afar."

"She's never been good with things like that," Ollie whispered conspiratorially. "I've always been much more into fairies than she is."

Annabelle stifled a groan.

"You know what?" he continued. "I think we could find a good holiday for you and your mum."

"Only for mammy," Heloise said sternly, "She needs to be away from me or her head will explode."

They exchanged a glance again. "But where would you go while she's on her holiday?" asked Ollie.

"I can be at home. I know how to make toast," she said, beaming proudly. "And when Mum has to work late or at night, Mrs. Browne comes and tells me to go to bed. She wouldn't mind."

"Wouldn't it be lonely to be home alone?"

"I play games in the window," she said.

"What sorts of games?" said Ollie.

"Sometimes, we look at all the people and make up stories of who they are. And sometimes, we look at the posters in your window and say where we want to go and what we would do on a holiday. Mammy doesn't always play with me," she hurried to add. "I also play it with Teddy and Mr. Periwinkle. But," she said, grinning over her hot chocolate, "Mr. Periwinkle is a chicken, and he *always* wants to go to Edinburgh."

Ollie laughed. "Why does he want to go to Edinburgh?"

"'Cause," she grinned, "he was hatched from a scotch egg..." She laughed at this pun the way only children can laugh at puns, but her laughter spread and soon they were all rolling with laughter.

When Heloise had left, thinking she was carrying a holiday in a white envelope, the pair didn't speak for a long time.

"So..." Annabelle said eventually. "What can we do?"

"I think we should go talk to her. Ask what she needs. Say that we'll help."

"Sounds like she needs professional help, though," Annabelle said slowly. "Not that much we *can* do, if that's the case."

"No... but before I start calling protective services or anything like that, I'd quite like to have more to go on than the words of a five-year-old. Maybe she's just exhausted and needs a break, or maybe she's basically a pill-popping mess like... you know."

"Yeah."

After closing, they went to the pub around the corner for dinner. Neither of them said it out loud, but they could keep an eye on the flat above the butcher's from there. It was a quiet dinner. Each of them thinking back to their own childhood and all the times their mother had wished herself away from them. They thought about the Christmas gifts they had hoped would please her, and how her mental illness in the end had gotten the better of her and they'd moved to their aunt's in their early teens.

"I'm sure it's not the same," Ollie said after a while, patting his little sister's arm. "This may just be a stressed single mother."

"I hope so," Annabelle said.

"Doesn't mean we shouldn't offer a hand, though," Ollie said.

"No. We should. If she'll let us..." They exchanged a glance that brought up a memory of a teacher coming round to theirs, offering help. It hadn't been a good evening.

"I'm sure it's not the same," Ollie repeated.

They waited until the light in the pink room with the dinosaur in the window went out, around eight, then waited a few more minutes before they walked up the narrow staircase from the backyard and knocked on the door.

The woman who opened it wore a beautiful sari and smiled at them.

"Yes?" She said.

"Are you Heloise's mum?" Annabelle asked, a little confused. Whatever she had expected, this wasn't it. She had half expected a copy of their own mother on the other side of the door. Someone dishevelled, worn, tear-stroked and dirty.

"Yes?" the woman said, suddenly looking serious. "Is something wrong? Has something happened?"

"Eh... kind of? Like... I don't know..." Ollie seemed as at a loss for words as his sister.

"Would you like to come in?" said the woman, holding the door open and offering them the warmth and yellow light of the hallway. "I'm Laxmi."

"Oh no," she said, holding her hand in front of her mouth. They each had a big mug of tea, and the conversation had hobbled its way through the story of the afternoon, and Heloise's worry about her mum being sad.

"It's true," Laxmi admitted, "I was crying almost every evening last week. It was my mother's birthday last Wednesday, and I... well... you know." They nodded. She had told them the sad circumstances of her mother's death, and how they hadn't spoken for almost six years before. Not since she'd gotten pregnant with Heloise.

"I didn't know she had seen me more than that once. I tried to explain that I was sad because her grandmother died, but I didn't think that she might combine that with the general tiredness and think I was falling apart. That's awful. Thank you so much for letting me know."

"We're really sorry," Annabelle said. "We misunderstood... It's just... with our mum, and the way we grew up... You know..." she said, and this time, Laxmi nodded. They had spent some time explaining why they had thought the worst. Why they'd been so worried.

"It is a beautiful thing for you to care that much about someone else's child," Laxmi said, standing up to give Annabelle a hug. "Thank you so much. I'm not going to lie, it's hard work being a single mother in the city, with a big job and a small network – but I'm okay." They hugged again.

"Listen, if you need a babysitter or anything... She could always come down to us in the shop, or I'd be happy to sit for a while after work if you'll be home late, or anything. Here," Annabelle said, handing Laxmi her business card.

"Thank you so much," the woman smiled. "I may take you up on that."

And she had. Over the next weeks, they met regularly. First, it was to help out, but Laxmi and Annabelle got on so well that soon, they were the best of friends. In almost no time at all, three weeks had passed, and the office had just closed early on Christmas Eve.

"You ready?" Annabelle giggled. Ollie looked as nervous

as she felt.

"Ready," he said. They knocked on the door and waited.

"Merry Christmas!" they said as Heloise and Laxmi opened and let them in.

"Oh, come in, come in, it's so cold, close the door!" Laxmi said, taking their coats and leading them into the living room. Heloise came running with Mr. Periwinkle, the chicken, and told Ollie three new egg puns she had made up herself. It had taken a little time for them to regain her trust after they'd ratted her out, but they had apologised deeply, and promised to make an even better surprise.

"So glad you could come over," Laxmi smiled, pouring tea into their mugs. "Heloise has made you something. Haven't you, Heloise?" The girl ran into her room and came out with a shoddily wrapped parcel, a huge bow tied slightly askew across the front.

"Merry Christmas!" she said, then stepped behind her mother, suddenly shy as the present was unwrapped.

She had painted them a picture. An unmistakable house – a roof, a chimney, two square windows and a door – on a green lawn, painted with quick, easy strokes. To the right of the house stood four figures. One small and three large. Heloise and her mother were rendered quite well, her mother's colourful sari separating her from the other large figures in the painting. The pink hair gave Ollie away, and Annabelle recognised herself in the bright red lipstick and long eyelashes.

"Thank you so much!" they both said, and complimented the style and likeness.

"She said it's her city family," Laxmi smiled. "It's different than her country family as there are no fairies in the city." They all laughed. They all smiled. Annabelle and Ollie had tears in their eyes.

"We've got something for you, too," said Annabelle. She pulled a huge white envelope out of her purse.

"What's this?" Laxmi said, letting Annabelle rip the top strip off, then stopping as she saw what was inside. "No... what's this? What... no...?"

"Disneyland!" Heloise screamed. "Disneyland!"

"You didn't have to..."

"We know," Annabelle smiled. "But we were talking about it, and we would have *loved* to go to Disneyland with our mother when we were kids. And this is the whole shebang!" Annabelle explained, fully aware that Laxmi could have afforded a full-works trip to Disneyland herself.

"We've pulled some strings and you're going to sleep in Cinderella's castle!" she said, looking at Heloise, who near fainted with delight. "There are princess makeovers, ride passes... all sorts of things..." She drew a deep breath. "And two full spa days for your mum," she said, looking to Ollie, still a little unsure how they would take the next part. "Massage, facials, foot therapy, a flotation chamber... Nothing but pampering for two days."

"But..." Laxmi said, confused, "What about Heloise?"

"Well..." Oliver said, winking at Heloise. "Annabelle always says how she would love a spa day or two. And I, for one, would *love* to have a princess makeover with you!"

"Yeah... We thought we could all go," Annabelle said. "If you don't mind?"

She looked at Laxmi then. Saw the tired lines around the eyes and how they were now pulled up with excitement. She saw how her shoulders had sunk at least an inch since their first meeting, just knowing she had someone she could lean on if she needed to. She looked nothing like their mother, Annabelle knew, but now she felt certain that Laxmi never would.

Lyrael's song

You may not believe this to be true, but it is true all the same: being an angel is actually quite boring. Lyrael had been an angel for thousands of years now, and all he ever got to do was swoosh around between the clouds and go to choir practice. It had been fun for a few hundred years, sure, seeing the world from above, circling in the thunderstorms – and he quite enjoyed singing. But why the archangels still called it choir *practice* was a mystery to him. With each passing centennial, it became increasingly clear that the concert they were practicing for wasn't going to happen any time soon. And Lyrael *wanted* it to happen. He had a song in his chest that had pushed its way forward his entire life. He longed to sing it. Longed to present it to the world. But every time he suggested it to the choir master, he was told it had to wait until after the concert.

"Let's get the important bit over with first," he would say, and Lyrael would sigh, and wait a decade or two before he tried again.

Well… perhaps they weren't the *only* things he got to do. If the archangels were particularly stressed and needed a fast flyer, they'd let Lyrael do a few message runs. He wasn't supposed to – he was a choir angel, not a messenger – but sometimes they'd let him, all the same. He'd been carrying messages of divine will to mortals all over the world, but decades upon decades passed between each one, so most of the time, Lyrael was bored.

Four times, they'd trusted him to do a soul run. Those were his favourites. He carried the frail, glowing, mortal souls from heaven and all the way down to Earth, finding the precise time and moment they were meant to be born. It was so exciting!

The first had been to a grand palace filled with servants. The expectant mother had been surrounded by helping hands and, as soon as the child was born, she was washed and pampered, dressed and groomed – ready to present the emperor with his new heir. The second soul, Lyrael delivered to a small cabin somewhere cold and frosty. The mother had been all alone, received the child herself and cut the cord. She'd fed it, wrapped it up, then pulled her boots on to go and feed the cows and the chickens, get some water and check on the pigs. Lyrael had stayed the night, watching over the little baby. It had looked so weak, Lyrael had wondered if he'd been sent on this run because the soul was so fragile it wouldn't make it anyway. The thought made him angry, and he'd wrapped his wings around the little bundle, keeping it warm and close until morning.

The other two times had been run-of-the-mill soul runs, but he'd loved them all the same. He enjoyed the importance of them. He enjoyed watching the silvery shimmer of the souls glow stronger and stronger as they got closer to Earth, and the quiet, lonely flight back home when he was done. He would sing, then. He would fly in big loops, taking the longest possible way back, and sing all the way home.

"Please, please, please, Maraphael," he said, "please send me on a soul run. It's been decades since the last time, and I'm *bored.*"

"There's choir rehearsal today," said Maraphael. "You're not meant to be going anywhere."

"All we ever do is rehearse!" said Lyrael. "I'm sick of rehearsing. If there aren't any souls to deliver, are there any messages? I'll take the smallest one you have. Anything!" He felt the song billow forth in his chest, and he knew he had to get out of here. He needed to sing.

"There are no messages right now," Maraphael said, annoyingly serene. "Please return to your section, Lyrael. I've got nothing for you."

"Fine," he said, a little more angrily than what was appropriate for an angel of the thirty-first section. "*Fine.*"

There was an unusual buzz in the air as Lyrael made his way back. Archangels were flying in small huddles, eagerly gesticulating. He overheard fragments of conversations, all of them excited and flustered.

"But I have a soul run," he heard one of them say. "I won't make it."

"I'm so sorry," another replied, "but what can you do?"

"Maybe I could give it to a runner?" the first suggested. Lyrael recognised him as Archangel Galanael, a recent promotion.

"You're really not supposed to..."

"But it's such an important..."

"Galanael!" Lyrael said, flying to catch up with them. "I'm very sorry, but I overheard your conversation. I'd be happy to take your soul run for you if you have other things you'd like to do."

"Really? You would?! Oh... eh... you..."

"Lyrael."

"Oh, Lyrael, you're an *angel*," said Galanael. The other archangels laughed, and Lyrael stifled a groan. It was just about the only joke you heard up here, and he didn't find it that funny.

"Just give me the ticket and I'll be on my way," he said.

"Here," said Galanael, and handed him the little golden ticket with the soul number on. "Thank you so much! I owe you one!"

Lyrael was ecstatic. When he saw Maraphael's face, it was all he could do not to laugh.

"I'm sorry," she said, "I still don't have anything for –"

"I've got a ticket," said Lyrael, handing it over like a golden treasure.

"This is a top-priority job," said Maraphael, narrowing her eyes and studying the ticket closely. "I'm not sure I can give this to you..."

"Galanael asked me to take it. He had somewhere else to be."

"I... I need to check with the higher ups," said Maraphael. She pulled out a gilded leather tome, flipped to an empty page and started writing in her graceful script.

May choir angel Lyrael, thirty-first section, handle the soul run for...

"Would you mind?" said Maraphael, noticing that Lyrael was reading along as she wrote.

"Sorry," he said, and took a few steps back, picking at his wings and brushing his robe.

"There's no reply," Maraphael said after what felt like a full decade had gone by. "They must be busy with... everything." She looked at Lyrael and sighed. "Fine, but this is a *really* important soul run. Please be extra careful, and go straight there. No... diddle-dawdle," she said.

"I promise!"

Maraphael clapped her hands, and a sound like glitter and bells filled the air. The soul was there, in Lyrael's hands, shimmering and glowing like the others had.

"Why is it special?" he said, studying it closely. Maraphael smiled.

"They're all special," she said, "now get going. It's meant to be delivered by midnight down there."

"Thank you!" Lyrael said, and started the descent.

It was a special night. He could see other angels shooting here and there across the sky, many more than would normally be out on a night like this. He tuned in to where he was meant to appear and felt a rush of heat as he entered the moment in time. He couldn't help noticing how bright the stars were shining, how quiet the fields were, how crisp the air. The soul emitted a faint warmth, pulling him in the right direction, guiding him to the place it was meant to be born. Lyrael slid between numerous houses, quiet and still, until he came to a simple farmer's home, right at the edge of town.

It was built in the tradition of its time. On the bottom level, the animals were kept for the night. Their damp, musky heat spread through the rooms as protection against the cold night air. Upstairs, there was a living space, a wide platform, partially divided in two. One part for the people of the house, another for guests and visitors. Lyrael searched the platform, but couldn't find a birthing mother among the dozens of people sleeping there in rows. *How strange*, the angel thought. *What are they all doing here? Has the entire extended family come to town?*

A noise caught his attention and he glided down to the first floor. And there, in the storage space next to the animal pen, in a corner, lay the girl he was there for. She was very young. A teenager. Her face gleamed with sweat and her black hair clung to her cheeks. An older man, perhaps her husband, held her hand and wiped her brow. She clenched her teeth and pushed in silence, aided by two older women of the house.

Lyrael stood quietly, and watched as the soul's moment grew closer. It vibrated in his hands, eager to enter its body and begin its life. It was strange, Lyrael thought, that the woman wasn't placed in the guest room. But as he waited for the birth, he flew through the sparsely lit room and saw again how packed it was. *Perhaps*, he thought, *she got here late. And it would be hard for her to squeeze in among the others up there. No, there's no room. Down here, at least, she can move a little.*

That's when he felt them. He felt them in the air, and in the wind, and in the song in his chest. The choir angels – they were all there. He slid to the window, saw the light of them out in the fields. So much light. There had to be thousands and thousands of them. The whole choir! The realisation hit him like a thousand bad dreams. The concert! The concert was happening tonight, and he was missing it!

He wondered if this is what the other angels had been rushing for. If Galanael had given him the soul run so he could join the choir. They had been talking about this concert for millennia – all the archangels and most of the messengers had made arrangements to they could join in too. Now, he would be the only one to miss it.

He was just about to leave – place the soul on the windowsill and fly as fast as he could out there. Catch the ending, perhaps, or at least get to see the choir in all its glory. But just as the thought struck his mind, he turned to the girl, and she stared right at him and she smiled. It was as if she'd expected to see him there. She wasn't the least bit surprised or scared. This young girl, lying on a thin coat on the cold stone floor, waiting for her first child to come to life in a place that didn't have room for her.

He closed his eyes for a second. Smiled back and held the soul gently in his hands. This was his job. This was what he was here for. The song breached his chest and, with the soul shining like a diamond beacon until it finally joined the newborn body, Lyrael sang.

The baby was beautiful. The mother swaddled him in cloth and placed him in the soft hay of the animal's manger. The only soft place in this hard little house. Lyrael watched them. He could leave now, but he didn't want to. This quiet stillness they shared, the three of them – the baby and his parents – was filled with nervous expectation, yet it was incredibly calm. It filled Lyrael's heart with warmth and joy, and he didn't care about the concert at all.

He just sang. He sang the songs of rejoicing he had been practicing for the last few thousand years. He sang the song of his chest, over and over, clapping his hands. He performed for the little baby and his parents, although they didn't seem to notice him.

"Ma'am," said a young boy, standing in the door. He looked excited and scared. He looked full of imagination. "Ma'am, is this him? The angels came to us on the fields and sang that the King of Kings had been born tonight!

They said to follow the star, and it led us here."

"This is him," said the mother, certainty booming in her voice. "And I welcome you in."

"It's here!" called the boy, waving to his friends outside. And so the rest of the night began.

They all came, just as it was foretold. Lyrael watched the shepherds enter, carrying lambs, which they gave to the newborn child. Archangels rushed in, sang and congratulated each other. They patted Lyrael's back and applauded him for a job well done. The mother and baby shone; the father held around them, protective, tired and proud. The night was filled with peace and magic. Lyrael sang and sang.

The eyes of the clockmaker's daughter

Giovanni de Camino was the best clock-maker in the world. It wasn't just that his clocks were more accurate than others – although they were – but they were also *wonderful.* People would come from all over town to look through his shop window, and the rich and powerful would send their servants to buy his creations as soon as they were ready. One month, that was Giovanni's rule. For one month, his clocks would stand in the window, free for all to enjoy, and as soon as that month had passed, he would pack them up in branded crates and send them on their way.

The King of England had one where a single red rose bloomed every evening at five o'clock. The Duchess of Hamburg – some say it was a gift from her lover – had one where a courtly couple met on a bridge at midnight. They would share a single kiss before tearing apart from each other, making their way back across the little pond. The Pope himself was said to have one of Giovanni's clocks,

where each hour belonged to one of the twelve apostles. At one minute past the hour, a silver door would open, revealing the apostle of the hour. Painfully slowly, he would move out through the door, kneeling in front of the clock to pray at half past the hour, entering a door of gold and pearl at fifty-nine minutes to the next.

If you asked Giovanni where he got his ideas from, he would laugh and say he had the most amazing muse sharing his home. His nine-year-old daughter, Adriana, was blind, but drew beautiful pictures with her words. Every night, she would tell him a story, and every morning, he would try to imagine how to turn her story into a clock.

Adriana couldn't remember her mother, who had died when the child was two. But Giovanni was a loving and doting father, and Adriana had never been left wanting for anything at all. Their house was modest but filled with incredible things. Giovanni had created a world for his daughter that she could explore with her fingers and hands. He hired the best schoolmaster in town to teach her science and arithmetic, and a nun came to help her with religious studies. Then, at night, when he closed his shop and walked upstairs, he would read to her from their many books before she, in turn, would tell him a story. Their life was a happy one, and they loved each other deeply.

The house was filled with Christmas. The clockmaker had made twenty-two little mechanical toys – clapping monkeys, slithering snakes, marching soldiers and braying sheep – and Adriana was busy playing with them as her father prepared their dinner. When someone knocked on the front door, Giovanni didn't hear it over the clamouring of pots and pans. He didn't hear Adriana step across the floor, or the creak as the heavy door slid open.

"Hello?" said Adriana. "Who's there?" The stranger stared at her milky eyes for a long time. He could have turned and walked away. The girl might not even realise he was ever there.

"I can hear the rain drip off your cloak," she said. "Your breathing's fast. Like you're nervous." She cocked her head to the side for a while, seeming to hold her breath to hear better. "It's a rattling breath," she said. "You are sick, or old, or both. Would you like to come in?" She stepped aside and held the door open.

"Papa!" she called into the rooms. "We have a visitor, Papa!"

Giovanni ran into the hall. He was always scared something would happen to Adriana. He called it his 'always fear'. It lay as a snake, coiled around his heart, and whenever something unexpected happened, it squeezed and squeezed and squeezed.

"Adriana!" he snapped, "You're not supposed to open the door!"

"I'm sorry," she said, "I got curious."

"Curious children have curious ends," her father said before turning his attention to the old man on the stairs.

"Master Mariscotti?" he said, confused. "What brings you out here on Christmas Eve? Come in! Come in, you are wet. Here, let me take your cloak."

The little girl had frozen in her tracks. Master Mariscotti didn't like children. *Everyone* knew he chased them with his cane, sent his dogs after them down the street – or ate them, if you believed Jacob Pirelli.

Her father led the guest into the sitting room, pulled up a chair in front of the fire and offered him some steaming broth to warm his heart and bones.

"So tell me, Master Mariscotti, what brings you out tonight, the night before holy day?"

"I'm not one for holy days," Mariscotti grumbled. His voice was hoarse and the short sentence sent him into a spell of rough, rattling coughing.

"You're not well," said Giovanni.

"I've been worse." The old man sucked his teeth. "I need you to build me a clock," he said.

"I see," said Giovanni. "Come by the shop in the new year, and I will..."

"No," the old man said. "This needs to be... This is a different clock. It shouldn't be discussed where your assistants or shop girls or customers can hear... The drawings... they should be kept very private."

"I'm sorry, I don't think I understand?" Giovanni said.

Adriana felt the hair on the back of her neck stand to attention, and slipped sideways until she found her father in the large room. She wrangled her fingers in between his, and tried to imagine what someone like Master Mariscotti would feel like. His skin would probably be cold and hard like a clock face. Smooth. Perhaps like stone, or perhaps like glass.

"I want you to build me the Black Clock," said Mariscotti.

Giovanni laughed. "Haha! You nearly had me there. Come now, Mariscotti, why are you really here?"

The old man hissed. "Curse you, boy," he said, although Giovanni was a grown man himself. "Don't laugh at things you don't understand."

"But the Black Clock," Giovanni protested, "you can't be serious. It's a fairy tale!"

"Doesn't mean it's not true, boy. There is much truth in fairy tales."

"Listen," Giovanni said, hearing the puttering from the food in the kitchen. "It is Christmas Eve. I'm about to celebrate with my daughter. I don't think this is the time..."

"What's the Black Clock?" said Adriana. The old man shot an uneasy glance at the girl. He realised she must have been there the whole time, but somehow, he hadn't noticed her.

"That's nothing for little girls to concern themselves with," he said, and started another round of coughs.

"No, it certainly isn't," said Giovanni. "Go play with your toys."

But Adriana could feel a story in the air, and there was nothing she loved more than stories.

"Won't you stay for dinner, Master Mariscotti?" she said, smiling her most endearing smile. She felt her father tighten the grip around her hand, but she paid it no notice.

"No, young miss, I should get back to my dogs and –"

"Won't you stay for dinner, Master Mariscotti?" she said again. Her father squeezed her hand then, hard.

"Don't be rude," he said. "Master Mariscotti has already said he needs to go."

"Yes... No, thank you, little madam. I'm afraid I can't stay for dinner," he said. He was shifting uneasily in his chair, and Giovanni's apologetic smile did nothing to reassure him. "Now, please leave us so we can..."

"Master Mariscotti," Adriana said.

"Adriana!" her father said. "Don't you dare..." But she had made up her mind.

"...won't you join us for dinner? It is Christmas Eve, and I believe the tradition says you cannot refuse an invitation three times."

The men sat stunned. These were superstitious times in a superstitious town, and Adriana had ensured that Master Mariscotti couldn't leave without cursing himself by his thankless nature.

"I would be honoured," he barked, so harshly that Adriana whimpered a little. But her father, knowing his daughter's heart to be a good one, decided to make the best of the situation.

"I am sorry, Master Mariscotti, for my daughter's rash

decision. But it truly would be an honour to share our Christmas meal with you, and perhaps share with you one of Adriana's many stories."

Mariscotti mumbled under his breath, a rumble and stumble of words they couldn't hear. Then he drew a deep breath – leading him to another coughing fit – before finally settling down.

"So, she's a storyteller is she?"

"I am," said Adriana. "I collect them."

"Aha. Know the one about the boy who fell in love with the moon?"

"I do."

"Know all the stories of the saints?"

"Of course."

"Know the songs of the apostles?"

"By heart."

"Know the one about the cow who couldn't drink milk?"

"Y... no?" Adriana said, "I don't think I've heard that one."

"Good," said the old man. "I made it up."

"Oh," Adriana said.

"Just wanted to see that you weren't a liar. Tell me a story then, little miss," said Mariscotti, "while your father makes us food."

Adriana was, despite her young age, a storyteller worthy of an audience. Master Mariscotti must have heard a thousand stories told in his life, but still he found himself laughing and gasping along with the little girl's words.

"And all was well in the dale..." she finished, just as her father came in to let them know the food was ready.

"Thank you, miss. That was a good story indeed."

"Had you heard it before?" Adriana asked as she made her way to her seat in the kitchen, touching her way along the counters and chairs.

"I had indeed, but never have I heard it told with quite as much life to the pictures. Tell me," he said, slumping down by the table where Giovanni held out a chair for him, "is it not hard for you to describe things you've never seen?"

"I don't know what everything means," Adriana admitted, "but I know what they should sound like."

"I beg your pardon?" said the old man.

"Sand, for example," Adriana explained. "I don't know what it is, not really. My father says it's like the fine dust on cobbles, but that some places by the sea, there are long stretches of nothing but sand. You'll burn your feet if the sun shines on it, but if you sink your feet down, the sand is cool underneath. And some places, deserts are made of nothing but sand. Burning, scalding, flying sand that whistles by your ear and rubs down everything it finds. I don't know what that means, but I know what it sounds like. It's dry and big and complicated."

"Is it now...?" Mariscotti nodded. Giovanni shrugged and grinned at him across the table. He was proud of his daughter's good mind.

They ate in awkward silence at first, but soon, Adriana's bubbling well of questions and the old man's longing for good company made the dinner a lively affair. The food was good, and Mariscotti – once he'd gotten warmed up by the meal and a glass of good wine – turned out to be quite generous with both his laughter and his stories.

"It is time for presents," said Giovanni when the last of the poached pears had been split between them and everyone had eaten two marzipan flowers each.

"For you, Master Mariscotti, I have nothing to offer but another glass of wine and some bones for your dogs," he said.

"Best Christmas present I've been offered in years," the old man smiled.

"And for you, my darling daughter, I've got something extra special." He placed in her hands a thick book, bound in leather. The pages were made of the best vellum; she could feel the fine texture under her fingers.

"What is it, Papa?" she said. "What does it say?"

"It says nothing," her father smiled. "It's for us to write down your stories." Adriana and Master Mariscotti gasped. Vellum was incredibly expensive. Spending such a fine material on writing down the words of an ordinary person. Who had ever heard of such thing?

"Oh, Papa!" she said, and reached for him to come over and hug her. "It's wonderful!" She pulled a small parcel from her pocket. "My turn!" she said, and handed it over. Giovanni opened it with careful fingers and found a whittled figure inside.

"What does it look like?" Adriana said, "I wanted it to look like a bird."

The two men studied the little figure in quiet contemplation. If you asked an artist to carve a bird, it would look nothing like this little statue of wood. But if you looked at it with the knowledge of birds – light in the air, feathers, flight, nests and eggs and fragile bodies – you couldn't call it anything else.

"Is it not good?" Adriana said.

"It is wonderful," her father said, and hugged her, as filled with gratitude as his daughter had been moments before.

"And for you, Master Mariscotti, I have a special story that has to be told under a full moon. Will you come back to us at the full moon to claim it?"

Giovanni held his hands out to the table, as if to indicate that the man would be more than welcome to come back.

"Thank you, little miss," Mariscotti said, "I think I shall."

"Now it's your turn," Adriana said.

"I'm afraid I didn't come prepared with presents," said Mariscotti, patting his pockets as if to emphasise the point.

"I wish for a story," said Adriana.

"Alas, I'm not much of a storyteller."

"If I wish for a specific story and you know it, will you give it to me?"

"I don't see why not," the old man said, not picking up on Giovanni's sudden suspicion.

"I would like the story of the Black Clock," Adriana said. The old man laughed until his laughter became coughs, and he coughed until he started laughing again.

"You are a clever one, you are," he said. "I'll tell you what. If your father agrees to build me the clock, I will give you three presents: first, its story; second, its drawings and schematics, straight from the master himself; and third... I can give Adriana something that would make her see better."

Giovanni and Adriana both went quiet. For a long moment, the two men eyed each other up across the table.

"It's a dark thing you're asking me to do," Giovanni said.

"It's a dark thing for me, not for you," Mariscotti said, "and my final gift will be of great value..."

"Papa," Adriana said, "don't do anything you oughtn't for my eyes... I am happy. You know I'm happy. I just wanted the story, I don't mind." But Giovanni looked down at his daughter, and he knew there was nothing he wouldn't do if it would help his daughter's sight.

"You've got yourself an agreement," he said, reaching out his hand to shake the old man's.

"And so do you," Mariscotti replied, and grinned with pure relief. "Well then! Are you ready for your story?"

Adriana could feel something important had happened,

but she was too curious to care very much. "I'm ready!" she said, and the old man began.

"In a country far to the North, there lived a king. He was a good king, kind and wise, and he ruled his kingdom by listening to his people – the poor and the rich alike. The King had two sons, who were born within the same minute on the same day. Although the first would be next in line to the throne, none had thought to make note of which one came first. The King had hoped it would show in time, which one had the royal traits. Then he could simply name that one the eldest, and all would be well.

"But people are fickle beings, and their personalities change like rivers and streams. As soon as the brothers were old enough to realise that one of them was destined for the crown, they grew fiercely competitive. By their 20th birthdays, they were each earls of separate holds, and everyone expected a civil war to break out as soon as the King died. The King was worried. A civil war would damage the kingdom, affect the people and make them weak to enemy attack. Even if he named one of the sons his successor, he doubted the other would keep the peace. He could pass his kingship to a rival family, but he saw none he'd trust with his kingdom.

"But the King also had a daughter, who was generous, kind and wise. The laws of the kingdom forbade her to rule, and although the King knew in his heart she would be a better monarch than her brothers, he didn't feel the kingdom was in a position to handle such a drastic change. But the daughter had a son who'd inherited his mother's kindness and wit. He was only five, but everyone who met him was struck by what a clever and charming boy he was.

"*If there only was a way*, the King thought, *that I could stay on the throne until my grandson is of age. Then the kingdom's future would be secure... I believe even his uncles would agree*. But the King was already old, and the winters were tough and long. Looking into his own future, he struggled to see another 13 years.

"One morning, an old magician knocked on the castle door, saying he had a solution to the problem nesting in the King's heart. He was granted an audience, and the King – although reluctant – agreed to pay the magician 30,000 silver coins if the magician could solve his problem. He let him work from the empty magician's tower in the castle for as long as he would like.

"The King was wise enough to put clauses in their agreement. The magician could not kill anyone, nor curse any member of the King's family. The magician scoffed at this, and said his solution would be one that would lighten the King's heart.

"'I will need some materials,' the magician said, and messengers were sent out far and wide to bring back coils and springs and hardened glass, copper threads and diamond cogs.

"The clock he built was pure black, and there were no numbers on its face. Instead, the King's life was written down in minute detail, inscribed with ornate letters and embossed in silver strands. Although it was a beautiful piece, it made everyone who saw it feel slightly uneasy.

"'It's fine work, magician,' the King said. 'But I fail to see how a timepiece will solve my problem.'

"'When you wind this clock and start the pendulum,' the magician said, 'Your life will reverse. Every day, you will be one day younger, and every year, you'll be younger than before. It will tick as long as you wind it up every night, but the day you stop, you'll only have 12 more hours to live before your time runs out.'

"'Immortality,' the King gasped, studying the masterpiece.

"'No,' the magician said, sternly. 'It is only a return of

your given time, once over. When it's done, it's done.'

"'Could you not build a clock that winds the other way?' the King asked, suddenly greedy with the prospect of eternal life.

"'I'm afraid not,' the magician said. 'This is a one-lifetime deal.'

"That night, the King wound the clock, and his heart made a single skip to mark the change in time. He wanted to live until he could pass his kingdom to his grandson, but by his grandson's 18th birthday, the king felt better than ever, and decided to remain on the throne for a few more years.

"Five years later, one of the twins waged a challenge against his father, and in the ensuing war, much of the King's family were tried for treason. The kingdom was in turmoil, so the King decided to stay on the throne until it was settled and strong. His wife died, his sons died, and when the clock had reverted the King to a mere 20 years old, he had no one but his grandson – now teetering on old age himself – left in the world.

"'This clock,' the King wept, as his 15th-to-last birthday came around, 'it has given me such power, but it's such a dangerous thing. Please,' he said, looking up at the man he now respected and loved like a father, 'help me destroy it.' And the grandson – now the patriarch of a large family of his own – promised to destroy the clock as soon as the King was dead.

"That very evening, the King signed the throne over to his great-grandson, as his grandson recommended it passed him by, and gave them his clock to destroy. He walked into the dark night, and stepped into the sea as his very last hour ran out. Two minutes past the hour, the magician – who hadn't aged a moment since he'd arrived in the castle – packed up his things and left the place too.

The kingdom finally had time."

Mariscotti ended his story, and Adriana and Giovanni both hung on his every word.

"But how can Papa build you a Black Clock?" Adriana laughed when she realised there were no more words coming. "That's a fairy tale!"

"I happen to know," Mariscotti said, "that the grandson trusted an old friend to destroy the clock. A clockmaker who knew everything there was to know about cogs and wheels and moving parts. But his curiosity got the best of him, and before he destroyed the Black Clock, he made a precise schema, noting down each of its little bits and inscriptions.

"That schema was passed to the clockmaker's son, who passed it to his daughter, who sold it to a merchant, who traded it in a bazaar in a distant land, where it lay buried in a chest of papers that were sold to an old collector in an auction last year. That collector," Mariscotti said, "had heard the story from an old magician, and knew what he was looking at as soon as he saw the chart." He stepped over to his cloak and pulled out a leather holster hidden underneath. Inside, there was a thin roll of parchment, and as he rolled it out on the table, Giovanni gasped.

"This is impossible!" he said, "the detail... the coils... that inscription...! I... hm... but, of course, with copper... and if we... yes... yes... it could be done..." he muttered, and Adriana could hear in his voice that he had fallen in desperate love.

For five weeks, Giovanni worked in his workshop all day, then turned the lights off in the shop and continued working at night. Adriana was the only one allowed to help, as she couldn't read the schema, but could feel the different parts and help him with the most delicate bits. Mariscotti came around almost every evening, watching the progress with eager eyes. Some nights, he would stay for dinner, and Adriana and he would exchange stories, growing closer every day.

"What are you going to do with that extra time?" Adriana asked one night.

"I am going to walk until I'm tired, then bury the clock somewhere safe. Then I will sit, hopefully somewhere beautiful, and feel my time run out," Mariscotti said.

"What?!" Adriana stood up so quickly her beaker toppled and spilled across the table. "You want to die?"

"Not yet, not yet, dear child," Mariscotti said, patting her hand and mopping up her water with his sleeve. "I can walk for a very long time. I want to see the world. I want to see more countries. I will live for a few more years, but I'm a very old man," he explained. "I have no wish to reach youth again."

That night, Adriana cried and begged her father not to finish the clock. But Giovanni kept thinking about Mariscotti's reward, wondering what Adriana's life would be if her eyes could only be healed.

"Tomorrow," Giovanni said, at the end of the fifth week. "Tomorrow, we'll be ready."

"Good," Mariscotti said. "I will get your reward in order."

When Mariscotti wound the clock, they all held their breath.

"I felt it!" Mariscotti said, "I felt the skipped beat!" And then, as quietly as he'd entered their life, he walked out with the clock under his arm. Giovanni looked down at the parcel he'd left behind, and carefully pulled it open.

Dear Friends, the letter read.

I thank you for these weeks and the clock you have built me. Enclosed, you will find the deeds to all my properties, signed and notarised letters transferring you my fortune, and a guide to my vast collection. However, I promised you a way to make Adriana see better.

Sell it all. Sell my houses, sell my collection, take the money and take her around the world. She should feel the sands beneath her feet, listen to the lion's roar and smell the spices of Zanzibar. Take her around the world, dear boy. Take her around the world.

Your friend,
Marvolio Mariscotti

Giovanni de Camino was the best clockmaker in the world. It wasn't just that his clocks were more accurate than others – although they were – but they were also *wonderful*. They said he had travelled the world with his daughter and brought wonderful stories home with them. And each of those stories, or so they said, was wrapped up in one of his clocks.

The truth about cranberry sauce

Don't tell them the truth about your cranberry sauce. Don't mention how you'd never even considered making your own until your favourite author posted his recipe online, and you knew you had to try. How even though his recipe was for plain cranberry sauce (half a kilo of cranberries, two cups of water, two cups of sugar) and he stated clearly that he preferred to keep it simple, you were outright rebelling from your very first try, adding orange peel and cinnamon sticks and experimenting with flavour.

There's no use talking about sugar. How two cups made it too sweet and one cup made it too tart altogether. How one and a quarter cup (if the orange is large and sweet) or maybe one and a half (if the orange is smaller, or the peel looks dry) is more than enough, and just right. The family likes it sweet or sugar-free, and you can't please both, so just keep quiet about the sugar. It's none of their business anyway.

Don't tell them that you add star anise. No one ever wants to hear about the star anise. They'll tell you – even if you only mention it in passing – about their hatred of all things liquorice (although star anise and liquorice taste nothing alike if you taste them carefully) or about that one time they got too drunk on Sambuca and puked liquorice-flavoured (star-anise-flavoured) vomit into their neighbour's shoes.

When the ruby red gloop is bubbling away, and you've skimmed off the pink froth with a spoon because you suddenly remembered you're supposed to, just sprinkle the surface with two star-anise stars. Just watch them twinkle and turn around in the depths of flavour they'll create, twirl and dance alongside the cinnamon stick and orange peel and occasional squirt of lemon juice. When you pick out the orange peel, cinnamon stick and star anise, dispose of them carefully, in secret, completely. Then listen as the family talks about the deep flavour and slight spiced tinge. They'll say it reminds them of something – they just can't put their finger on what.

Don't tell them how cranberries make you worry about your role in the planet's demise. How the punnets say the berries are grown in the U.S. of A and packaged in the Netherlands, and now they're here and you're supposed to pick out and discard the soft ones. You do, of course, but the pile grows larger than it should and you wish you wouldn't have to dispose of these berries that have travelled across the world, setting surprisingly deep carbon footprints for such small berries indeed.

No one needs to know how you keep some of the soft berries in, because you're not sure it matters, and it somehow makes you feel less guilty about tossing away the rest. Then, when the jam is half done and most of the berries have burst, you get half into panic thinking that the few that haven't are the soft berries. That they're bobbing on top with their bloated flaws, ready to burst in your mouth with poison or gas or some long-forgotten plague. Don't tell them you burst the last berries with the back of your spoon, so no one will think they're bad.

When they've stuffed themselves with turkey and stuffing, and oohed and aaahed about your cranberry sauce, prepare for the recipe questions.

"It's just half a kilo of cranberries, two cups of water and sugar to taste," you'll say, then smile. "And whatever I feel like putting in. I think, today, I used some orange peel, a cinnamon stick..." and just as they're about to turn their attentions onto something else, you'll smile again and add, "and star anise." And then the conversation gets going, but in new ways now that they've already eaten.

Now, tell them the truth about your cranberry sauce. How you'd never even thought to make your own until your favourite author posted his recipe online, and now you've made it your own. Tell them how you never mention the star anise until after the meal, as they all say they hate it when none of them do. They'll laugh and ask if anyone knows where cranberries grow, and you'll wish you'd brought salad instead.

My cranberry sauce

500g cranberries
2 cups of water
1⅓ cup of sugar
Orange peel of 1/2 large orange or 1 small (go for peel that looks soft and juicy. Shiny is good. Dry and cracked is bad)
1 small cinnamon stick
2 star anise
A splash of orange juice or lemon juice, or none at all

1. Boil until it's done. You'll never know until you get there.
2. Skim of the pink froth when you remember. Just leave it if you forget.
3. Do the water test (drip some jam in a cup of water and see if the drop holds its shape) until the sauce keeps its shape, but then give up when you realise it never will, and just stop when it feels like it's time.

Acknowledgements

When I was little, there were so many stories that belonged to Christmas. My understanding of the holiday was firmly anchored in the Christmas gospel, but took wide and frequent trips into mystical, magical lands. Papa Panov cobbled shoes, Marte Svennerud adopted children, Ajaks and Hector bravely fought wolves, and the steadfast tin soldier was… well, steadfast. This is a heritage I carry with deep gratitude, to the authors who wrote these stories and to the family members who read them aloud.

My kind and generous wife is my favourite audience, the person I always write for, and the one who inspires me the most. Thank you for being all that – and for being my unwavering editor, master of layout, personal assistant, life coach, and manager, too.

Thank you to Emily Clapham for dancing into my life on watercolour fairy wings, and illustrating this collection so beautifully. I cannot wait to mystery-project along with you again.

12529376R00113

Printed in Great Britain
by Amazon